Trouble Cove

by

Nancy Lindley-Gauthier

Trouble Cove

Cover Art by *Debbie Taylor*

The Wild Rose Press, Inc.
PO Box 708
Adams Basin, NY 14410-0708
Visit us at www.thewildrosepress.com

Publishing History
First Mainstream Historical Edition, 2017
Print ISBN 978-1-5092-1413-6
Digital ISBN 978-1-5092-1414-3

Published in the United States of America

I stood alone on the deck

of the sturdy little craft. The sea rolled and roiled, bigger and bigger from one moment to the next. I should have been afraid. We had every chance of sinking this little pleasure craft out on this wild sea. Terror should have touched my heart.

Instead, I stood alone, poised between ocean and sky and felt, quite ridiculously, free.

Brent's *The Ship* poem fluttered into my mind, all uncalled for, with its odd parallel between shore and death. I felt alive. Like listening to divine music, I lost myself in what was both a long time and a short time; endless, yet, wanting it to never end.

Michelson struggled the length of the deck to check the sail. I couldn't spare a moment to watch him, but I knew he took some pains over the boom.

A tiny orb glimmered in the distance. Could it be a harbor light? It faded almost at once. Still, I scanned what I could see of the island. The shoreline was no more than a hulking gray shape in the dimming daylight.

Surely, we would see the lighthouse's bright beam soon? I was sliding past exhilarated and heading toward exhaustion. I had no real idea of the distance we had come, though I could clearly envision a map of the coast we sailed.

We journeyed up the east coast of Cape Breton Island, the northern tip of Nova Scotia. We needed to sail by the lighthouse south of McLellan's Harbor before we turned to enter the harbor itself. It would be a trick to bring the boat around at the exact moment to glide into the mouth of the harbor.

Dedication

For Kent, like always

Prologue

Cape Breton Island, Nova Scotia
Late autumn, 1916

...a horrible war embroils Europe. Canada has already leaped into the fray by sending men, munitions, and even food. Though we every day fear invasion ourselves, for most of us, life remains curiously the same. Yet, I cannot say any of us remain untouched.

Chapter One
The Thistle

Thistle dove bow-first into the heart of a white-capped wave. Foaming water rushed down from the transom, straight over the cockpit, and straight over me, clutching the wheel.

"Steady," Michelson, momentary captain, as it were, shouted over the howl of the wind. Calm, and utterly in command.

I gasped, drenched and freezing, but didn't respond. Steady was simply impossible! Mr. Michelson might act like we were a young couple out for a jaunt around the bay, but I was not used to screaming up and down monstrous, white-crested waves. I white-knuckled the argumentative wheel of the sailboat to keep our course.

Michelson scrambled lightly around, double-checking the ropes on the heavy boom before he gave a quick look to the mast. Then he threw a long length of rope at me.

I jerked back and glared. If I'd had a free hand, I might have tossed it right back at him.

He didn't pause or bother to explain. He grabbed up the trailing end and fastened the long loop of rope to the mast and then threw the line over to the side. A precaution then. No doubt he expected one of us to wash overboard any moment. The trailing line of rope

2

might offer one chance for a rescue.

Perhaps, it might be better to avoid any thought of 'overboard.' I pinned my gaze on the white-capped ocean swells before me.

"You're meeting them just right." Michelson brought a pair of binoculars up and gazed ahead. "The trick will be tacking east at the right moment." Even with his deep, resonating voice, the rest of his comment was lost to the storm.

Neither of us knew the *Thistle,* built by Halifax's best and raced all summer by the wealthy socialite Avery Brookeson, very well.

Earlier in the day, when Avery, with his polished drawl, had said, "you go get the boat harbored then. I'm not spending my day on the water," to our delivery man, I had to step in. This Michelson fellow delivered fish up to the hotel kitchen, for heaven's sake, and spent his days running a dory, dragging nets, or whatever the local men did. What on earth would he know of fancy sailboats, to say nothing of sailing through storm? He might be young and strong with an intriguing, sharp-eyed gaze but, er… Oh dear, I discovered I was gazing at Michelson like a love-struck school-girl.

Avery had scowled at me. He treated me like I was general help, but I was the manager's assistant, not his.

"Avery, what are you thinking?" I had argued. "Surely, we can secure *Thistle* well enough here at the dock?"

"There isn't much time." Mr. Michelson had jerked his head toward the front window. "If she's to be moved, it will have to be now."

Avery had crossed his legs and bent, fussily straightening the cuff of his pants. The dawn's red rays glinted off his sterling silver watchband. He never cared what trouble he put people to, or what risk he asked them to take. He didn't look at Michelson as he spoke. "I'll see you get a tenner if you anchor her up safe in McLellan's harbor."

"Ten!" If I'd had one of the parasols any nearer, I'd have clobbered Avery with one of them. "You spent more on the wine for that boat's delivery party this summer! Why, it's practically brand new, and you can't even be bothered to take care of it!"

Avery had lolled back in the soft chintz of the day room chair. "Wine is an excellent point, Elizabeth. You should definitely take the horse and trap to Ingonish for a few incidentals. Organize a storm party. You can be my date, you lucky gal."

"I'll take the boat to safe mooring." Michelson had growled. "I'll hike back down the island road tonight and collect my money."

Looking back at the exchange, I felt anger all over again. Stupidly, I had run out the door to help Michelson. The angry sea whipped up white caps, even then. The pennants on the little vessel had fluttered madly as the darkening, slate blue horizon promised worse to come.

I should have hung back, should have used some reason, but I did not.

My impulsiveness was completely to blame for my current circumstances. Cape Breton Island's coast wasn't littered with shipwrecks for no reason. I had never before met the wind full-gale nor been so far from shore.

I pointed the nose of the *Thistle* at the high spot of each wave and clung on as we flew up and up as if we would slice through the very clouds above. *Thistle* plunged over each crest only to dive again and again.

The hours drew on and the blue-green ocean swells grew mountainous and the day darkened to an early night. Still, a competent sailor sails from this moment to the next, and so we did. Michelson left me the helm as he secured and re-secured the little vessel. He kept a sharp watch out for rocks and shoals, besides.

He wore the raingear from the hold; Avery's gear, I guessed. I had a huge shapeless sou'wester over my day dress and was too busy to feel the cold.

Thistle did not make speedy headway, yet we did gain north steadily. The waves carried us alongside the craggy coast. The boat dipped and bowed, but Michelson had set the tiniest reef in the low sail and kept us moving.

We plunged over one more massive wave. I dared to think we were getting there.

"I don't care for that boom stay," Michelson shouted. "I'm going below after more rope. Safer to sure-secure it."

I stood alone on the deck of the sturdy little craft. The sea rolled and roiled, bigger and bigger from one moment to the next. I should have been afraid. We had every chance of sinking this little pleasure craft out on this wild sea. Terror should have touched my heart.

Instead, I stood alone, poised between ocean and sky and felt, quite ridiculously, free.

Brent's *The Ship* poem fluttered into my mind, all uncalled for, with its odd parallel between shore and death. I felt alive. Like listening to divine music, I lost myself in what was both a long time and a short time; endless, yet, wanting it to never end.

Michelson struggled the length of the deck to check the sail. I couldn't spare a moment to watch him, but I knew he took some pains over the boom.

A tiny orb glimmered in the distance. Could it be a harbor light? It faded almost at once. Still, I scanned what I could see of the island. The shoreline was no more than a hulking gray shape in the dimming daylight.

Surely, we would see the lighthouse's bright beam soon? I was sliding past exhilarated and heading toward exhaustion. I had no real idea of the distance we had come, though I could clearly envision a map of the coast we sailed.

We journeyed up the east coast of Cape Breton Island, the northern tip of Nova Scotia. We needed to sail by the lighthouse south of McLellan's Harbor before we turned to enter the harbor itself. It would be a trick to bring the boat around at the exact moment to glide into the mouth of the harbor.

Thistle jauntily swung up a great swell. I looked for the red-trimmed lighthouse. The storm so darkened the late-afternoon skies that I could make out no more than vague shadows.

At the peak of the next wave, finally, I caught a glimpse of a flickering light. "McLellan's light," I shouted. Without planning or thought, I leaned into the wheel.

Michelson lunged over next to me and helped me bring her around. We were a tangle of arms and legs, both trying desperately to drag the wheel left against the pull of the current. His enormous strength made the difference. The boat started to come around.

I looked again for the light, but saw, instead, the

roofline of Widow Trumbull's house, clearly lit and shining brilliantly into the face of the storm. Her lights shown day and night this last half-century, or so it was said.

Mrs. Trumbull, forever vigilant, forever hopeful and…too far south.

"No," I screamed. "We're still south of the harbor!"

I jerked back on the wheel without regard for waves. Michelson mirrored my efforts, and somehow turned the *Thistle* away. She started to heel sharply and crept up the next massive comber almost sideways, but luck smiled on us. The sturdy little vessel leaned terribly, then righted.

"That wind and waves could speak!" My companion shouted Wordsworth's words at the sea. "Too close, too close the boundless deep!"

"Not too close," I shouted right back at him. Our voices carried on the screaming wind as if we'd become part of the storm. Who was this fisherman, this man who shouted poet's lines at the raging seas?

"I thought I saw the point lighthouse," I gasped. "Only then I saw Mrs. Trumbull's! I might have killed us, there on the rocks."

"I thought I saw the lighthouse, too." He stood by me with one hand lightly on my waist. He likely meant to help me keep my balance, but my heart flip-flopped, and I caught my breath. 'Doubt not love at first sight, for I recalled the day our eyes first met and…'

Oh, great stars! I had to keep my mind on the sea!

"I know McLellan's Light," I choked out. "I won't mistake it again!"

I inched aside to offer him the wheel.

Gruffly, Michelson said, "No, miss, keep to your station. You're a better sailor than I. We both mistook the light."

At his words, the chill of the freezing salt spray disappeared entirely. The wind and waves were as nothing. What man ever stood aside for a woman, no matter how competent?

I looked around in all directions. "We can't be far from the lighthouse beacon. We'll both see it and agree this time, before we pull her around. We need to pull her around quickly, as we risk a knockdown."

"Lead the way, Captain." He flashed me a wicked grin.

Captain!

The unceasing roll of the waves threatened to flatten us if we made the slightest mistake. I could not ignore the fact that if the boat went over, we would both drown in the frigid waters. My lack of concern was foolish, and yet, I fought down a ridiculous desire to sing. If fear wanted to visit me as I stood there at the helm, my companion had utterly banished it.

Who was this Michelson, our fishmonger, our all-sorts delivery man?

He stood tall even among his fellows, bearded like most but somehow apart. He strode with confidence, whether on land or sea.

We had barely exchanged two words all summer, though I had noticed him weeks ago. I had been setting up the ballroom for a dance, and he had brought in a delivery from Ingonish.

Oh, who could imagine! It had to be my ridiculous, whimsical nature. Only I could stare into a stranger's eyes and find both wisdom and humor. Only I could believe I saw past the handsome visage and look straight into his soul.

He'd made his delivery as I stood, frozen and speechless. We'd gone our separate ways, but I could not escape the thought of him. The deliveryman! My mother had not wrangled me a position working among the swells for the summer, only to have me chase after a deliveryman!

Yet, I had. If I made myself be honest, I had risked my life, not to fetch this charming boat to safety as I pretended, but for this one chance to stand beside him.

"The light," Michelson abruptly growled. Indeed, the steady, yellowy light that marked the harbor's rocky point shone faithfully through the dark and mist. It was unmistakable.

Thistle started down into greenish water of a deep swell, and I knew the other side of this monstrous wave would be our opportunity. I braced myself for the attempt, glanced up at Michelson, only to find him smiling down, most curiously, at me.

All unplanned, I smiled up at him.

He seized the wheel around either side of me. "Now!"

Together we brought her around, between heartbeats it seemed, but more importantly, in-between the monstrous waves.

After that, although the sail still did not go easily, time passed all too quickly. We rode the *Thistle* into the sheltered harbor, triumphant.

I slowly climbed onto the weathered pier. I did not want to leave this day behind. A part of my heart had sailed away, somewhere out there, on the thunderous, gray-black sea.

Chapter Two
Dinner

Avery swung the dining hall door open and stepped back to allow the French lady to enter. She was followed by another hotel guest, the smarmy Mark DeLaMore, and then some gentleman from down around Halifax.

After the boat, and moments of—what? Terror, joy; I don't even know, but after the extremes of it all, the awful fear and then finding myself sailing triumphant into the wonderful little harbor beside Mr. Michelson, after walking for ages in the drenching rain, after all of it, dinner seemed silly.

I, the 'Captain,' had battled the sea with a madman, shouting and laughing into the gale. We had conquered.

Now, I stood back, hands folded politely, and waited for my betters to be seated. The glittery light of the chandelier, the perfectly appointed dining table, the ladies in their finery, the white flowers a staff person must have brought back from Ingonish while I was out struggling with the wind and the waves all brought a sense of the surreal.

On the other hand, I still felt my everyday irritation at the mere presence of Avery's cohorts. The various gentlemen guests were sons of the wealthy, drinkers and gamblers for the most part.

Mark made a point of holding out a chair for me.

10

I swept over in my high-necked evening crinoline and allowed him to assist me as if I were one of them, one of the genteel ladies. What a farce.

Avery settled his mother, Mrs. Brookeson, and the French lady at the table opposite. He looked a bit peaked. He wore a gray jacket, as there was no black-tie pretense these days, but he looked rougher than usual. He had probably spent the afternoon with a bottle.

He glanced my way and arched an eyebrow. "Looking lovely this evening, Elizabeth." Ah, the master seemed inclined to forgive my little mutiny.

Genevieve Grayson and her sister Ariel floated in, divinely dressed as always, and the gentlemen fell over themselves to assist them to their chairs. The gents were less solicitous of the older ladies, but that was also commonplace at this point. We few had been together for weeks, since most of the guests had left.

The kitchen girl, Beryl, balanced a soup tureen carefully as she came down the length of empty table. No actual wait-staff were left at Oceanside. Mr. Osten, our manager, frowned at poor Beryl, who all but dumped the soup in an effort to skirt way out around his chair.

The French lady, Madame Catherine Chatillon, wrinkled her nose at the rich aroma wafting around. We were given to understand such common fare beneath her. Quite likely, we were ourselves beneath her.

We set to slopping up the broth from the very fish Michelson delivered this morning. Had that been only this morning? I could hardly believe the events of today were, indeed, today. A year might have passed since dawn.

I peered into the inky darkness outside our

windows and remembered when Michelson had turned his far-seeing gaze southward. "The sky grows heavy; the storm is upon us…"

Wouldn't he think we all looked ridiculous if he stood outside this window right now and gazed in to see us, gathered with such false cheer? This party hall could seat nigh onto a hundred. Here, we dozen sat and ate in a ridiculous pantomime of grander peoples and busier times.

I might even now be dead, drowned and frozen at the base of those rocky cliffs. Yet, I sat and genteelly supped my soup. If Michelson hadn't managed to turn us away from the false light, I would not now be sitting here. What could that strange imposter light have been?

There had been something wrong about it. Something terribly wrong.

I found I was simply sitting, staring at my spoon. I had made a horrible, nearly deadly mistake. My mistake. Still, I didn't quite see how it had happened. I wished I knew someone to ask. I had seen a flickering light to the east, plain as plain.

None here at this ridiculous table would know about such things. Nor would my adventure be viewed as appropriate dinner conversation.

I looked at each of my dinner companions, one after the other. I knew them all as well as one can get to know people over the course of one summer. That is to say, they were strangers. One summer, what is that? I might never have seen them before.

We dozen should not still languish here, weeks after the scheduled closing of the grand hotel 'Oceanside.' Nova Scotia's lovely Cape Breton Island had been the stage for our magical summer, but summer was long behind us. The curtain should have dropped by now; we should have returned to our real lives.

"Mrs. Brookeson?" Genevieve leaned over the table, nearly dipping her front frills in her broth. "I've ordered a few warmer clothes from home, but my sister here insists we'll be on our way before I have need of anything very heavy."

Mrs. Brookeson didn't so much as glance at her. "I have no intention of departing. My youngest is overseas in this miserable war in Europe. I will not step one foot into my own home until he returns." She shot a look at Avery. "I thought I had made myself perfectly clear."

"Of course, Avery did tell me so." Gen smiled. "I'm honestly pleased to stay, although of course I realize it has been terribly difficult for you."

Mrs. Brookeson bit back whatever snappy response came to her. Recently, she had become very polite to Genevieve. I found it odd. Mrs. Brookeson had seemed nothing but impatient with her, all summer.

Avery smoothly said, "I'm sure my father is working out a way to recall him." His words could not be true. One did not recall soldiers from battle on so little cause. He lies, I thought, he lies.

Genevieve murmured, "None of us are in a rush to leave. This place is simply delightful."

Another lie. Nothing delightful remained at the resort. No summertime diversions carried on into fall. Without central heating, the oversized Victorian-style house was already uncomfortably cold. Colder every day. No one stayed because it was 'too delightful' to leave.

Gen carefully did not glance at Avery, for that indeed would give her reason away. If she wrote this play, her final scene most definitely involved a white gown and a trip up the aisle.

We all smiled as if it were, indeed, too delightful to contemplate departure. Were we nothing but a pack of actors?

Avery Brookeson remained to support his mother, as surely his days of playing 'the wealthy host' here at Oceanside were quite done.

The French lady persisted in presenting an air of mystery. The war in Europe raged on and suggested the obvious answer. She must be a refugee of sorts, though she never explained. A wealthy refugee to be sure, but avoiding the war nonetheless.

As for the rest, they were society and mostly the adult sons and daughter of the wealthy. They could do what they pleased, but why did it please them to remain at a summer resort well into chilly autumn?

Here we sat and shivered in our summer-time finery. Pearls and puffy half-sleeves were our costumes. Our lines were derived from magazines for the most part. Everyone expressed opinions on this season's fashions, as if there were no other cares in the world. All this elegance, from fancy dress to shimmering chandelier, might be no more than costumes and props.

Conversations washed over and around me without my taking part, while I puzzled over our odd circumstances.

A choice of haddock with dill, or drowned in Hollandaise sauce provided the main entrée. Ariel and her sister Genevieve tried to discuss a famous Parisian café with Madame Chatillon. She pretended she did not understand them. Ariel slipped smoothly into French.

Madame raised her eyebrows as if she could not

understand that either and murmured "le accent."

She never wanted to talk to anyone.

Osten offered a tray of sliced breads to Avery, then leaned a trifle close to him and in a low voice, said, "Two gentlemen in the smoking room." Avery gave a curt nod and went back to rapt attention at whatever Genevieve was jabbering about.

Two louts, no doubt; some pair of fools that Avery had enticed to make up numbers for poker. Avery would keep his poker night a secret. He kept up a gentlemanly profile for Genevieve.

He didn't care if I knew about the boozing and the gambling. In fact, he glanced at me and smoothly winked. Ah yes, he'd like me to fetch some of the resort's booze in to the party later, no doubt. I sighed, but nodded. All part of my job. I was supposed to assist the manager, Osten, but most often, I waited on Avery.

Avery must have felt my gaze still upon him as he half-turned as if to speak to me.

Genevieve abruptly handed him the plate of breads.

I stifled a laugh. If only she knew that my mind was filled with remembering the bravest sailor in all the world! I had no designs on a spoiled rich boy; no, none at all!

"Another evening without any entertainment." Mrs. Brookeson barely finished eating before she started impatiently from her chair. The older ladies followed her lead, setting aside their forks and following her to the front room.

I said nothing. If I brought in cards, she'd snap and say there were too few players for a hand (and certainly wouldn't want me to join in). If I offered to do a reading, she would snarl about my lack of theatrical ability. For no good reason, it seemed like she'd started to detest me these last few weeks.

The younger set, all my age, wandered to the foyer directly after dinner. They were already gathered in a tight circle when I escaped the dining hall.

I sank down on the carpeted stairs of the front hall and listened to their bubbly voices. Ariel and Gen were central. The pretty gal up from Ingonish giggled at something Avery said. Did she guess she was invited only to round out the numbers at dinner?

I wrapped my thin-threaded, fancy-looking shawl tight around my shoulders and listened to the little party chattering.

Avery's low voice came clearly, "You'll have to believe me," followed by another flurry of giggles. The cousins, Doraleah and Edith laughed at anything he said, so one needn't imagine he'd said something clever. They so hoped to catch a man from 'good society.'

I was as good as a friend when they needed something. So 'not quite,' so actually 'the help' when it came right down to it. Mark stepped to the threshold to shut the door, raised an eyebrow in my direction.

I shook my head and waved him away. I didn't need some last minute invitation. They carried on as if having fun, there in the chilly foyer. Was this the very best of their day?

The very best of my day had been earlier. In fact, it had been at the turn off of the high road, when Michelson had said, "I'm glad you sailed with me, Captain.'

"Captain!" I wrapped my arms around my knees and leaned back against the stairs, remembering. How my heart had pounded when I realized I had almost turned *Thistle* onto the rocks. It was nothing to how my heart had pounded when the big, dark-eyed man called me 'Captain.'

Chapter Three
A Day at the Inn

"No need to dawdle about," Cook snapped.

I ignored her and puttered around the tea cart, checking and re-checking the spoons, the sugar dish, and then the spoons again. I had to pretend I wasn't waiting about on purpose. Pretended, even to myself.

Cook bustled around at the stove. She sighed heavily. "Do put that kettle back on the heat for me then. Mugs are right above."

I stretched up for the mugs warming on the stove's top shelf. I didn't mind helping out. The summer's half a dozen kitchen helpers had all gone now. Constantly trudging back and forth must wear on Cook's old legs.

"Not these?" I held up the clunky mugs. Cook would never serve any of the resort guests the common blue ceramic mugs. She nodded, and I didn't argue but gave them a quick rinse in the oversized sink. Busy work.

Without any sort of notice, Mr. Michelson, our deliveryman, my yesterday's sailing partner, shouldered open the huge side door and swung a wooden crate up onto the counter. He nodded to the cook. "Mrs. Buxton." He swung back toward the door and then stopped short at the sight of me.

He looked so astonished; I giggled. Then hastily I pressed my hands over my mouth.

Cook snorted at my silliness. "Pour the man a cup of coffee then. One tablespoon sugar, one tablespoon cream."

Ah, the reason for the big mugs. He came nearly every morning, I knew, but I hadn't guessed he stopped long enough for coffee. I fumbled around with the sugar jar, tongue-tied.

In a deep rolling voice, he said, "Thank you, Captain." The mug looked tiny in his hand.

I had to make a real effort not to giggle again. Honestly.

He leaned against the end counter and spoke to Cook. "You made it home all right yesterday?"

"No waves made it over the road, but the sea came as near as it needed to be." Cook shot me a look and realized I didn't have my wits about me enough to remember to pour her coffee, too. "Mine is plain black."

I poured hers and then a cup for myself too, as if I ordinarily joined what must be their morning ritual.

"Daro, all the bakery I ordered is never in that one crate?"

The man nodded. "It is. All they'd send. There's an outstanding bill."

Cook tsk-tsked. "I needed the lot. There's no help left here. I must get all the breads and cakes brought in." She looked at me. "You need to get after Mr. Osten about these bills, Elizabeth. We'll not have happy guests if we run short at mealtime."

"Yes," I murmured. *Daro*, I was thinking 'Daro.' What a strong name, like one of the great heroes of legend, a name of strength, but one with courage and kindness, too. I tried not to stare at him but, heavens above, you could imagine him as the hero in any story.

"Of course, they'll be paid. The Brookeson's are wealthy," Cook asserted.

The big man looked down at his coffee. "There's a current out there today, so I brought all the goods up by road. Stopped by here on my way down to Ingonish and borrowed the hotel's horse and cart. I don't expect it will be easy to make deliveries here much longer."

"It's early yet, surely?" Cook looked anxious.

"Hotel was supposed closed at the end of summer," he said. "I expected to be boarding up the doors two months ago."

"Boarding up?" I repeated faintly.

"Closing for the season. It can't be long, now." Cook busily set out the several loaves of white bread and canned fruits along the counter.

If the missus was to be believed, we'd not be leaving anytime soon. I didn't say it aloud, though.

"No telling how long before we see real weather." Daro sipped his coffee. "There's nothing but open beach here."

"I know it Daro, I know it," Cook fussed. "Nothing to stop the seas coming right up onto that fancy porch out there. Still, these engineers from far off must have known what they were about when they built the place."

He made no answer, and I finally ventured, "I'd just as soon stay for good." The strong coffee about took the fur off your tongue, which must be what made me feel so giddy. I could hardly think of one sensible word to string after the next. I, so noted for smoothly assisting with sticky conversations!

Our hero, I meant, the deliveryman; no, Daro, of

course. Daro shot me a piercing glance. "Tell me, Captain, that light yesterday. You remember the light we saw, shy of the point?"

"I'm so sorry. I can't think how it fooled me." I wanted to crawl into a corner. "We were looking for the point light for such ages, then suddenly—a light. It was a stupid mistake."

He shook his head. "I saw it, too. Where no light sits. I walked the coast below McLellan's this morn and found a few bits of burnt wood carried back in at the top of the tide. Can't imagine why someone would have been burning stuff out there, in the midst of storm." He set his mug on the side counter. "There's something not right about it."

'Not right about it.' I heard him say the words, but they didn't give me any chill, didn't tell me his suspicions. I didn't cast my mind over old tales or poems, which might have offered some warning.

"Fact is, more than half the lighthouses are dark now," he said. "Part of the war effort."

"That's as it should be," Cook said. "Keep the enemy's ships from using our navigational beacons."

"Yes." Michelson frowned down at his coffee cup. His dark curls fell forward over his ears, and a thin line creased his forehead as he thought. The muscles in his forearms tightened.

"Are you thinking the light might have been a signal light to the enemy?" Cook hissed.

Oh, everything people spoke of these days had something to do with the war. It was as if every motivation, every effort was tangled up in some confusing political plot. Did enemy ships lurk off our coast? Were German soldiers poised to invade? It couldn't be. Surely, the enemy had more than they wanted, fighting in Europe.

"I don't think so," Daro said. I waited, full of hope, but he didn't mention our sail, or say anything like how pleasant it was to see me today, nor mention meeting again.

I hardly knew what to say. I couldn't find the glib words I so easily chattered to Avery's sort of man. Mr. Michelson's thoughts seemed more important, somehow.

Cook discussed the number of guests she had to feed this week, and what needed to be brought in, and all the while I sat perched on the corner stool, smiling in what probably seemed a silly, schoolgirl-ish way.

Daro and I managed no other conversation.

I watched out the side window while he stumped back down the path to the road and caught up the big bay mare's reins. Too late, I thought I might have asked him about poetry. He certainly knew his Tennyson.

Cook snorted yet again when she turned and caught me looking after him.

"No use setting your cap for the likes of Daro Michelson. Every bit as arrogant as his father was, and a loner to boot." Cook nodded almost to herself as she pulled items out of the crate. "I saw him gawk at you. That yellow frock suits you fine. I don't guess you're wearing it by mistake, neither. I don't imagine he's used to running into the likes of you."

"He saw me all day yesterday in a huge old oilskin coat." I hoped I sounded casual. I began to set out a tray for luncheon. "What do you think he's worried about?"

"Storm. Like he said, it can get bad here. We've had years when wind and waves and sand came right up and over this stretch of road. There's likely to be blowing snow. There are stretches of coast road made impassible every year." She glanced at the huge beam running up to the ceiling. "I'm sure this building will do well enough."

"We all know winter storms," I said. "It isn't like I am from all that much farther south. There was all that worry about the light we saw, too. I wonder what he's thinking?"

Cook stomped across the kitchen. "Heaven knows. It was nothing but arrogance, taking that boat out yesterday. Him so sure he could outrun the storm."

"We did."

"You forget about Daro Michelson. You go ahead and make up your mind to marry one of these swells. You're more than a match for any of these society gals here. No need to spend all your days as poor as a church mouse." She echoed my mother, near enough.

The noon bell rang, and I scurried out the side entry with the tray. Beryl hustled in from the foyer where she had been tidying the sitting room.

"The front room is cold," she squeaked. "Them ladies won't want ter' sit out there today."

"Where else?" I asked. All summer we served out on the front porch. Late season though it was, it all still looked ready for a party, with white wicker chairs, swings, and settees arranged just-so, but oh-so cold. We'd switched to the front sitting room weeks back.

If the sitting room felt uncomfortably cold now, where could I put them? The dining hall echoed with emptiness, and the kitchen wouldn't do at all. I couldn't think of anywhere better, and again set up the trays in the front, where the sky-high windows overlooked a perfectly stunning view of the ocean.

Perhaps Mrs. Brookeson would remain upstairs. She'd be the only one likely to complain.

People often wandered into the midday buffet in twos or threes and served themselves. Today, not one living soul waited for the breads, cold sliced brisket, pickles, or jelly tartlets. Cook would be fit to be tied if they'd all gone off Ingonish for lunch at the one pub there.

Almost as I had the thought I heard Old George's fine Russell Motorcar purring its way into the drive. So there had been a trip to Ingonish. I hoped Mr. Osten had settled George's bill. There would be hell to pay if the old gent stopped showing up to chauffer guests around.

The sisters alighted together, and Genevieve handed George a tip. Two for lunch, anyway. I heard voices as the old art professor ushered the French lady down the front hall stairs; four then.

I withdrew into Osten's tiny side office off the foyer as they all went in to the meal. I was near enough to assist with any problem, yet not obliged to join the conversation. Bills needed attention, apparently. I began to sort the pile.

We of the resort enjoyed the popularity that went with spending.

Locals in the little harbor towns around us took the sudden arrival of this new resort in stride. While the reports from Britain were grim, the summer of nineteen sixteen would very likely be remembered for its local economic boom. The resort ordered everything imaginable, from vegetables to baked goods, fish to fine fillets, wine and brewed goods, and hand-made gift items.

I sighed over the array of bills stuffed wildly in the ledger book. I could only shake my head; our popularity certainly depended on our paying what was owed. It seemed Mr. Osten had not sent out checks with any regularity of late. An oversight? It had to be.

Genevieve leaned in from the front foyer.

"Is there anything I can do for you?" I half stood, ready to run out on an errand, if she required it.

She brought a finger to her lips. I could hear deep voices from the smoking room next door but could not quite hear what they said.

Gen winked at me. "The sweet shop lady set aside some Jordan almonds for me. Avery's favorite. I wanted to slip them into the smoking room when the men weren't about. It would be such a lovely surprise. I can't manage it, though. They'll notice me."

Notice her! I guess they would. Today she wore a burnt-orange mid-length jacket accessorized with a ghastly bright blue headscarf. She had no idea of colors matching or not matching, but her sister usually managed to dissuade her from truly wild combinations. I tried not to stare at the scarf. Tried.

"I can pop it in there later," I offered. "Did you want to leave a little card or something?"

She giggled. "No no, it can be anonymous. He'll enjoy them so, after dinner." She pressed the box into my hands and paused there, for half a second. "Elizabeth, you have always been so kind and helpful. I do hope you've enjoyed the stay here, too?"

So not only was Genevieve lovelier and richer, but she was, by miles, a nicer person than I. I forced a little smile and said, "It has all been lovely."

I trotted down the hall and peeked into the smoking

room.

Avery was bent over his wireless contraption. "I've had a broadcast right here in this room, word for word what was being announced in New York City at the same time."

Two guests rolled their cigarettes around and nodded. The one studying a coastal map did not as much as lift his gaze. The older one had a sharp look about him, not inviting conversation. I fairly scurried away.

I ran straight into another guest; Gen's sister, Ariel, also hovering, rather oddly, outside the men's smoking lounge.

Ariel had the same fate hanging over her head as I; make a good marriage and hurry up about it. Gen's not-quite-as-lovely sister spun and pretended to be looking toward the front foyer windows, as if she had been watching the gulls hover over the retreating tide all along. "We're so near the water; this hotel is almost floating on the sea."

"Yes. Lovely view." I tried to scoot by her. Why did she tarry here? I wanted my own lunch, if the guests were finished.

She followed like a pesky child. "I have loved this picturesque setting all summer. Now, all I can say is I'm freezing to death. Why isn't there a fire set in the fireplace? Thick wool drapes in these front rooms?"

"I'm so sorry." I stopped. "Can I get you something, heat your tea, or find you a sweater?"

"I'd like some information." She crossed her arms. "Have you worked for the owners long?"

"Only this summer."

"Tell me." Ariel fiddled with one of those very

insufficient curtains. "Exactly how has Avery avoided conscription into war service for so long? He's the perfect age to be in the service. There must be some reason?"

"I haven't any idea," I replied. I had every idea, in fact. The moneyed sort like Avery did not get packed off to war (unless their father wanted them to go, which might well be the case with his brother Daniel.) I certainly couldn't say such a thing, though.

Ariel stretched a hand to me. "Forgive my questions. You must be careful what you say, of course. But I want you to be perfectly frank. Avery seems quite the mystery."

"Thinking of him, are you?" I whispered, knowing perfectly well she was not. Practical, plain Ariel did not have the net needed to catch the likes of Avery Brookeson.

"Gen is. You know she is," Ariel spoke frankly. "Avery is popular in the Halifax social scene, and I guess he'll follow his father in their Halifax business. My sister is down to inherit a decent fortune and she's... Well, she thinks they are made for one another. I think we need a more practical approach." She tucked her arms all the tighter said, boldly, "More than once I thought him sweet on you, Elizabeth."

She plainly didn't mind what she said to the help.

"I'm not down to inherit anything, decent or otherwise," I admitted. "My family is nothing in the city, and if my sister hadn't married Ambrose Belanger and got noticed in the social pages, I probably wouldn't have even been hired here."

"If we had known you'd win all those ladies' sailing races, all of us would have tried to get you to come up and join our teams this summer. You were a lucky third for Avery." she trailed off and wandered to the sitting room.

I followed along after her. I could hardly ignore that she spoke not only frankly, but kindly. "I couldn't afford to stay here as a guest. This is my job, but I'm grateful you lot included me so much."

"Avery included you," she corrected.

"We are about the same age, I think." I shrugged. "Genevieve shouldn't give it a second thought."

"She doesn't." Ariel gazed straight at me, earnestly. "She doesn't ever have second thoughts. She thinks he's a perfect gentleman. Mims and Dad think he's perfect for her. Otherwise, we wouldn't still be here, would we? Hoping that their, er"—she waved a hand—"friendship might become more. More of a formal courtship."

It was exactly what my parents hoped for me. Oh, not Avery Brookeson, precisely, but that over the summer, elbow to elbow with the swells, they hoped I might make a match almost as good as my sister's.

Mamma had as much as said so, one afternoon, "After all, your sister is hardly the looker in this family! If you put your mind to it, who can say?" My toes curled up at the memory.

'Marrying Avery doesn't sound appealing to you, does it? Why? Is it Avery? Do you object to his lifestyle?"

"What? Oh, of course not. That is to say, I can't speak to his lifestyle. For goodness sakes, Ariel, working here is the most exciting thing I have ever done. I'm just not eager to find myself all settled down, in a house on a street exactly like where I grew up, with a view of other houses, and see nothing but streets and nosy people all my days!"

"I might have said the same thing myself, not so long ago." Ariel seemed poised on the verge of sharing something about herself, then abruptly barked. "You can't blame me for thinking there's something odd about him, sitting around here so late in the season. They delay returning to the city because of him, don't you think?"

"He's keeping his mother company and overseeing the resort. Mrs. Brookeson insists she's not going home until her younger son is released from service. You know how she is. She says her husband never should have signed for him to go in, a year under age and all."

"Unlikely reason, don't you think? I don't believe it," Ariel said. "Her husband probably hasn't the power, even with all their money, to get the boy out of the service."

"What else would be the point then?"

"I think Avery is avoiding service. Military service. I think his mother is staying here in order to keep him here. Away from the city, out of the public view. You know."

"Avoiding? Oh, surely not. It would be a—a shameful thing," I cast about for some other answer. "Surely not."

"I read about politics, the war, about people struggling for their lives, and then, here we are, acting as if the big society lifestyle was the most important thing in the world. You wouldn't know there was a war on, living here." She leaned forward and clutched her hands together. "Elizabeth, young men from all of Canada, Newfoundland, even here on the island are shipping overseas, some never to return! There's talk of German warships off this very coast and our merchant vessels go missing too often to be accidents. Yet, we sit around and talk about fashion. Organize teas. Do any of the rich young men here at the resort end up going off to fight? Does it seem like we are surrounded by patriots here?"

"Some here are very informed. Madame Chatillon is always pouring over the newspapers," I pointed out. "Avery and his cronies listen to reports on the wireless."

"He's more interested in the weather, if you ask me. He did nothing but host parties this summer. So frivolous. Making small talk about nothing. At home, we were very involved in our local Red Cross chapter. I was hoping we'd get back to doing more good works, this fall. Now, I'm stuck here as Gen's chaperone. She doesn't want to leave Avery. He's been dawdling here, weeks and weeks after Oceanside should have closed."

"Yes. What does that prove though? There are a number of us still tarrying here."

Ariel settled on the settee, automatically adjusting her skirt and smoothing her hair. "Yes. We all do have our reasons, don't we? Gen's reason is plain as plain. She stays for him, so I keep her company. Mark and most of the other young men follow after Avery's endless parties. They probably do the same when they are back in Halifax, hanging around all the clubs. Mindless."

"Mindless," I repeated.

"Some do have a reason to stay. I mean, our French lady likely has nowhere else to go."

I nodded. "And, the old art professor would

happily freeze to death to keep painting his precious seascapes."

"At the very least, wouldn't you think Avery would have been expected to be back in the city, by now?"

"None of my business," I mumbled.

"It is mine, if my sister is to marry Avery. I think young Daniel Brookeson got into a bit of trouble and they shipped him off, and his departure provided a handy excuse. Avery is no patriot and a coward."

I sidled down the hall, horrified. I mean, I might harbor some suspicions, but… "I'm so sorry you feel that way."

She stomped along in my wake. "Don't you see? If I could do one thing right by my family, I'd like it to be making sure Gen lands someone nice, someone worthwhile. She deserves it. If you know something about him, tell me."

I inched toward the front room in hope of escape. Honestly! What could I say? Then too, I did not want the resort Manager Osten overhearing me in discussing such things.

Ages later, I slipped into the smoking room and dutifully dumped the almonds in a candy dish. The room was in disarray, with furniture shoved back and a big map laid out on the floor. They'd marked the resort's beach as well as the bigger moorings, from Ingonish and McLellan's Harbor, past Meat Cove and around the point to Trouble Cove.

They'd strewn the mail on an end-table. So careless! Someone had grabbed up a letter for Madame Chatillon and left it in among the gentlemen's mail. I pocketed it with a mental note to leave it in the ladies' basket in the foyer. I noticed the headline on *The Cape*

Courier and with Ariel's comments in mind, paused to read the top article.

In the 'Over the Wires this week,' column, meaning the telegraph wires, reports of damage to a Marconi Telegraph station at the port city of Sydney. Signal was lost between Sydney and the Halifax station for much of two days, wire discovered down. Investigation has proved inconclusive; speculation blamed German sabotage.

They blamed every problem these days was "German sabotage." I never knew what to think of such things. The war seemed so terrifically far away.

I sat in the big leather chair and glanced around the smokers' lounge: the men's room of course. Wasn't it strange that I, just by dint of being 'staff' could wander practically anywhere in the establishment, without comment?

I sighed. Once I'd have thought it an extraordinary freedom. Now, I recognized it as a difference, an important difference, from me and the ladies.

Chapter Four
Threat of Storm

Thunder rumbled the morning to life. Sea spray and rain spattered against the windows, and the air tingled with expectation.

Even in my back-of-house bedroom, I could feel the wind shaking every beam and rafter. I scrambled out to the front hall window. Giant, white-capped waves stormed up our beach. Let my Daro be safe, I prayed. Fishermen knew when not to go to sea, I hoped.

I belted downstairs straight to our big monster kitchen.

"Missus Buxton ain't come." Beryl busily poached eggs on the giant stove.

"Cook hasn't come. Why, she's never missed a day." I drew back, aghast. Why in months and months, and indeed, in the face of thunderstorms and summer gales, she had always arrived precisely on time. Beryl could make breakfast and I could serve, but the idea of Cook not arriving suggested weather conditions quite beyond the ordinary.

The side door burst open to none-other than a drenched Daro Michelson. "Get you things. We need to get you inland."

Beryl gawked at him. "Ain't leavin.' I'll lose my job!"

Daro shook his head sending a shower of frozen

raindrops about the kitchen. "Who will do the cooking and cleaning here if you and Mrs. Buxton don't? They aren't going to dismiss you. You'll be safe up to your auntie's cottage, for now, anyway."

I nodded. "If he thinks you should go, Beryl, why then, you must go."

"You, too, miss." He motioned toward the coat rack. "Dress quick now, and I'll see you up to her Auntie Alma's, as well."

"Cook will be furious if she gets here to find no help at all," I said.

"She'll not be coming." Daro spoke with perfect assurance. "White squall. Boats are staying at their moorings, people are keeping indoors. "

"I must tell these folks then. I mean, the manager and all must be warned."

"We've told them," he barked. "We warned them months ago. This place was not built for a Nova Scotia winter. They insist it is 'state of the art.' We'll leave them to it. No need for you to stay. Get a hat. Freezing spray coming across the road. It might get bad here."

Beryl paused on the doorsill, looking at me. She wanted my permission, I realized. "Yes, go on, get your coat, run along. Breakfast is all set. I'll tell Mr. Osten I've sent you."

"Captain." Daro raised his eyebrows.

"I cannot simply up and leave," I hissed at the man. "There are still nearly a dozen guests here. There is the resort's old Packard." Even as I said, it, I guessed taking the big, open-topped four-seater automobile might not be the best idea. Still I carried on. "We could fit everyone in and get them to safety if you think we absolutely must leave."

"There's freezing spray coming over the road. It would be the worst thing, trying to take an automobile out. These rich people decided to stay here and now for better or worse, they'll have to stick it out. You come with me."

I had the feeling he'd have shove me in a rucksack if I didn't agree.

"I need a minute." I ran 'round to Osten's office, trying to think of some way to explain my departure, but Osten was not in his office. The smoking room also sat empty, and Avery's heavy overcoat had gone.

The wind rattled the windowpanes in the front room. The cold swept over thresholds and around doorframes and swirled around my feet. I stopped, abruptly, looking at the sea spray blowing from the little bay directly onto our wonderful front view windows.

Daro thundered after me. "Come away from the glass, miss!" He shepherded me back to the kitchen. His hand sat gently at my waist, and I fear my mind insisted on picturing him as my dance partner. Oh, if only Daro had been my escort at the summer ball. We would have swept out onto the floor as naturally as we sailed the *Thistle*.

I could see us together so easily. Daro would have said, 'Captain, I've never seen the likes of one who dances as well as she sails.' In response I would have said, would have said... Even my impressive imagination could not keep me on the dance floor as we shoved open the swinging door to the kitchen.

Beryl stood poking at the great stone oven. She looked guiltily over her shoulder. "Just checkin' the lucky cupboard."

I had no idea what she babbled about and struggled not to feel annoyed with the girl. It was hardly her fault if we were not, in fact, in an elegant ballroom. "We should pack a few things."

Though Daro's hand on my waist remained gentle, he nearly shook with urgency.

"Never mind," I said to her. "We'll go right now."

Daro hustled us out the door. "I'll show you to Alma's, but we must hurry."

Wind caught my hair and my cloak the moment I stepped over the threshold. Wind swirled in every direction, swooping from the rafters above while rolling in like waves from the sea. Instead of going to the road, we turned inland and dashed up the long hillside.

I glanced back only to see the resort's big bay mare standing, tail to the wind, watching me depart.

"My goodness. Ainslea-mare! No one's seen to her!" I started back.

"Miss." Daro Michelson pointed after Beryl. "Run along with Beryl. I'll close the mare in her stall and be right along. Go."

I hated leaving the big bay lady, though. One of the workmen usually filled her hayrick of a morning, saw to her water, and gave her a proper breakfast of grain. I worried Daro wouldn't know to feed her.

"Give her hay." The freezing wind stung my face and eyelids and I could hardly tell sea from land, beyond the outline of our lovely Oceanside. Stormy sea whipped right up to sky, and clouds raged right down to sea. I followed Beryl up a long trail out back, through the wide field and over a footbridge.

Daro Michelson caught up as we scrambled up a grassy hillside.

"It's a fast-moving squall, common enough this time of year. Might be bad, but it should over in a day." He plainly believed the 'might be bad' to the core of his bones.

****

Beryl's auntie lived in a little cottage tucked into the base of a hill, a snug eddy against the forces of wind and weather. She surprised me, for she could hardly be much older than I. She swung wide the door and shouted 'Welcome, welcome," before we were across the dooryard.

My fisherman settled us there and turned to depart.

"You aren't going back out into the storm?" I gasped.

He paused, his broad shoulders nearly filling the doorway. He reached out and just touched my arm. Softly, he said "My mum will be worried. I'll be able to get there okay."

I wanted to cling to him—to assure him his mum would most want him to be safe! I did not allow myself to do any such thing. My mind might be entirely fanciful, but I well knew how to appear quite sane and competent. Daro and I were scarcely more than strangers to one another. I could hardly, with any decency, confide my real feelings. I could hardly acknowledge them to myself. I said the first thing to pop into mind. "I wanted to discuss how we both mistook that one light for the lighthouse."

He paused in the doorway with the storm whirling around him. "Later. I'm afraid there's no way to say, not with surety, not yet. There's something not right with it. A false light."

His words were grim, and my heart sank as he

spoke. 'The false light,' must mean something, some dark thing, far more than I could imagine. I stood in the doorway and watched him rush back toward the coast.

The cottage was little more than a room, and I hated to intrude. Hesitantly, I made for a corner chair. Alma Doughty wasn't one to let someone sit uncomfortable in her home, though. She about dragged me to a chair in her warm flagstone kitchen, next to the old-style bread-oven built into the fireplace. In no time, we had lovely cups of peppermint tea in hand.

"I haven't felt so warm in weeks," I had to say. "Thank you so much for taking us in."

Alma chortled like a girl. She seemed few years older than I. "I am so glad of the company! I took my little boy over to play with his cousins early this morning. Thought I'd be here all day, all alone." The wind howled, but the Auntie's home was more than equal to the day. The wind was pleasantly muffled, the cold held firmly at bay. "My husband Donnall is down at the docks. He'll wait the storm out there, I'm sure. This looked like the most boring day, ever."

I snuggled into the deep armchair and thought it likely to be the most restful day I had had in months. I'm embarrassed to admit, I didn't spend a moment thinking how terribly cold and uncomfortable Oceanside was likely to become.

Beryl, Auntie Alma, and I started to chat about recipes and cooking and all.

"I'm so glad the Michelson fellow thought to bring you, too." Alma clasped her hands together and smiled.

"Cook thinks he's sweet on 'Lizbeth." Beryl smirked.

"Oh stop," I said.

Alma paused, hand-on-hip and glanced toward the door as if she could still see him there. "He's an odd one."

Beryl snickered. She could be tiresome, at times.

Alma sent her a sharp look. "Mind, my Donnall thinks the world of him. Says he's a worker. Still, the folks do say he keeps to hisself."

"Oh how funny, you have a little blue stone on your bread oven," I said, to change the subject. "Our Cook, that is, Mrs. Buxton, keeps a blue stone by the warming oven, too."

"For luck," Alma murmured. "You didn't leave it, did you? You must carry your luck with you."

Beryl looked stricken. "Mrs. Buxton leaves it there every night!"

Alma winked at me. "Superstition."

"Luck," Beryl corrected. "It works, everyone knows it."

"How do you know this stone is lucky?" I patted the one on the hearth.

Beryl giggled. "All the blue stones are lucky. There's only a few real ones in all of Cape Breton."

I looked at Alma.

She pulled a face. "That is the legend. The real ones are said to be pieces of CarnGorm, from the north of Scotland. They say the blue stone monuments on the north of the island all came from the same place, way back. Carried by the first settlers."

"Lots of people say they're real." Beryl put one fingertip on the little rock. She had a firm, if childlike belief. "I find lovely big scones in the tea cupboard above the one at Oceanside. Mrs. Buxton says the stone is lucky for me."

Alma nodded to the little brick oven and winked at me. "Scones, you say?"

The conversation returned to recipes, and most importantly, to party food. Bannock bread and pies, and then pies and how Alma's handsome Donnall sang at many a Ceilidh, or folk-music party, because he had such a lovely voice.

"Is your Daro much of a singer?" Alma paused delicately, eyebrows raised.

I had no idea. I'd heard him shout poetic lines at a raging sea but never sing. I could only shrug.

"I thought you'd know," Alma said. Beryl giggled and blushed. Whatever stories had Beryl carted up here?

Alma leaned forward and all but whispered, "You can hardly blame him if he's a bit of a wild one, now. People can say what they like, I say he's a decent fellow."

"Too different," Beryl piped up. "Cook says our Miss Eames comes from a proper city family and got educated like a lady. She's meant to take up with Mr. DeLaMore and live in Halifax."

"Tut," Alma shushed her. "The families obviously prefer this Mark fellow, but there is no telling a heart, or a pair of hearts, is what I say."

I am afraid I sat open-mouthed, completely floored. Mark? He came from good family, not with the Brookeson's sort of money of course, but he'd be expected to carry on in whatever his family business did, and he'd be looking for an educated wife. In short, exactly the sort of man my mother dragged me to various parties to meet.

Wait. How had Alma known Mark's first name?

Beryl said 'Mr. DeLaMore.' Alma had never even visited Oceanside. I glanced at Beryl, and she flushed with embarrassment yet again. Beryl had already been installed at Oceanside when I had arrived. I clearly recalled her hanging about doorways, even then.

"Whatever have you been saying?" I muttered, as I recalled my first day at the resort.

I recalled my mother chatting with Mrs. Brookeson in the front room on the day. She had marched in and said something ridiculous, like: "I'm confident this summer here will play an important role in our Elizabeth's future." I sure hadn't wanted to listen to my mother's plans for me but had dashed off to explore the magnificent Oceanside.

As both of our families hailed from Halifax, the ladies were already acquainted, even if the Brookesons were a clear social circle or two higher than us Eames. They must have talked about me and my, (my own face flushed at the thought) 'prospects.' And here sat Beryl, who so often listened at doorways and knew all sorts of gossip.

I could have sunk into Alma's saggy old sofa and disappeared entirely. A young lady's prospects! Mark DeLaMore! All the staff had probably known about the matchmakers' plans. Had they been chatting about how soon the romance would kick off, behind my back? How had I not heard any of this rumor, before now?

Alma kindly took the conversation back to mixing dough and other such things, but I am afraid I managed to contribute nothing more to the conversation.

Eventually, the storm blew by, and Beryl and I were able to wend our way back through the high meadow, over the hill and back down the sloping hills to Oceanside.

The bay mare stood with her head out over the top of her stable door, watching us struggle home through the wind-whipped grasses. I thought her a friend, but suspected it was all carrot-love from her side. I feared Beryl was much the same; a friend to my face, but a gossip when my back was turned. She plainly spent every spare moment at Alma's, sharing news from Oceanside.

The mare was likely my best prospect for friend, after all!

Chapter Five
Avery's Hair of the Dog

The following day arrived curiously quiet. The calm after the storm? The sun's rays glittered off the waves still rolling up onto the beach, and our artist was out there, painting the water and ignoring the rather more dramatic scene behind him.

The storm had shattered the front room windows. The sea had breached the inadequate seawall and left shells and debris scattered right up to the porch steps.

The hotel's builders plainly hadn't planned for a true Cape Breton-style winter storm.

Cook arrived very late in the morning, chauffeured by our manager, Osten, in the hotel's open-seat touring automobile. It had to have been a miserably cold ride, but he said nothing about it. He gawked at the shattered windows as if such damage were unimaginable.

"Waves left sand and flotsam right up over the road. We were lucky to get through to here, at all." Osten gawked at the sandy debris left on the porch stairs.

"You weren't here?" I knew he hadn't been but couldn't help but ask. I wanted to hear his explanation. How could he have simply been away?

"Held up in town." The manager stomped about the front room, staring at the damage. Glass and bits of debris littered carpet. The chairs were damp and a puddle still sat in the middle of the coffee table. The pretty lamps on each side of the room had fallen and the lampshades were sodden.

"I guess Avery must have been caught somewhere, too?"

"I didn't see him." Osten hastily marched up the front stairs to survey the foyer. "Probably stayed overnight at a friend's. Best to have Beryl sweep up in here straightaway. I'll have to order boards to cover these windows. This is unexpected."

"You hadn't planned on boarding up anyway?"

"Boarding up? Oh, closing. Closing!" Osten turned away abruptly. "I am much too busy to worry about something a long way off yet! Now, you go see to the, er…kitchen. Have Cook serve a quick brunch in the hall. I'll leave it to you to reassure the guests. I know I can rely on you to be tactful, Miss Eames." The hotel manager hurried into his office.

I found Cook tsk-tsking as she walked about the kitchen. There was no storm damage out here, but the hotel guests had been a bit of a storm themselves. Dishes and things had been left all about the kitchen.

"Had to fend for themselves, with only bread and jam, cold sliced meat, and the eggs and whatnot Beryl made. I see those two pork pies I had done ahead are gone." Cook sat heavily in one of the kitchen chairs and surveyed the mess.

I started clearing up the teacups and scattered flatware. "Did you expect this storm then?"

"Daro warned me about a storm brewing, what with the wind out of the nor'east. I've told Mr. Osten I'll not travel on such a day." She leaned back, frowning. "I've the dough set to rise, but blessed if I'm not about done, already. My legs pain me so, this weather."

I could not, for the life of me, remember seeing her sit down before.

"I can get the potatoes into the pot," I told her. I glanced over at the empty warming oven. "Was it quite a drive up from Ingonish?"

"I guess now I'd say Daro was right to worry. The road could have just as easily been blocked. And to get here and find windows shattered and all. Lucky no one was injured." She saw my gaze fixed on the lucky stone. "Daro saw to you and Beryl then? He said he would fetch you up behind the hill. The sea is too near here, too near."

I noticed she didn't mention those clever engineers or builders from 'far away,' this time.

"There was no real harm," I said.

"Could-a been. I can see Daro was right. Maybe now the management will take some proper care." She jerked her head toward the hallway, and I guessed she meant Mr. Osten or perhaps the Brookesons in general.

"Daro came all the way here from Ingonish during the storm to take me and Beryl to her aunt?" I busied myself setting up dishes that didn't need to be seen to for hours yet.

"Ingonish? No, likely he'd come down from his mother's there in the village at McLellan's Harbor, I expect."

"So, he doesn't actually live too far from here?" I thought of him, storming down the narrow coast road when he sensed a bad nor'easter coming.

"Not far, if it could be said he 'lives' anywhere at all." She shot me a look, sighed and carried on. "He's a wild one, child. I think he sleeps rough, wherever he happens to be, often as not. Not the fisherman his father was, but then, he hasn't inherited his father's big fishing vessel nor the money to run a crew, nor learned on the ocean as his father did, now has he?"

Oh?" I busied myself at the counter. She usually didn't share so much. I hurried around so she would see there was no need to get up and set to work.

"Yes, my yes. Mike Michelson made a name for himself from here to the George's banks. Right up until he set off into the teeth of a northern gale one November."

"Another November."

"Yes, nearly the same time of year as now. Nearly the same sort of storm. He was handsome and dashing and so proud. Everything about that man was proud. He brought in swordfish from far off shore, far far off, then. The story goes, that one November, he swaggered around the Purple Carp Pub and let everyone know his boat was heading back out, even though the rest of the fleet saw fit to cower in the cove. He wouldn't heed any of the other men. He said he'd stand the cowards a drink when he got back." Cook started to her feet. "He's not made it back yet, these many years."

"I'll do this," I hurried to say. I wanted to keep her talking. I motioned to the chair. "Rest a minute."

Cook, leaned back, shook her head dramatically, and carried on. "Left his pretty wife and children without a dime. You see what arrogance will do? When neither Mike nor boat nor his great haul ever came in well, his wife Daisy had nothing. Brought her children to her mother's place at McLellan's harbor. Daro, the oldest, got sent off to the Sydney mines, and him no more than ten or twelve at the time."

"The mines."

"He made a good job of it, by all accounts, working in the mine. Ten years or more. He left it without a second's thought, the moment his mother finally gave him leave. She wanted help at home you see. It's why he's not in service now. Supports a whole family of younger brothers and sisters."

"To think he grew up in Sydney, far from home, working all waking hours in a deep dark mine."

She wiped her hands on her apron. "Mind you. He's cut from the same cloth as his father. Brash. He'll come to the same sort of end, thundering off alone, unwilling to accept help or advice from one living soul."

Brash and arrogant? Surely she couldn't mean the man who had said, 'you're a better seaman than I, Captain.'

Cook prattled on, telling me my business, or what she thought it ought to be. "Young Mark DeLaMore would be much more suitable. They say he has a city job lined up. He'll have a nice house and spend summers in a place like this. You'd not want for a thing."

Suitable? I snorted. Wife of Mark DeLaMore. I could never consider such as him. A city house on a city street and always trying to impress the neighbors. I knew enough about that life. I snorted again, in a manner to quite match Cook herself. I tried a friendly, conversational tone to get Cook back on point.

"How long was Daro working in the mines?"

"I'd think it nearly ten years, he worked there in Sydney."

Ten years in the dark, dreaming of the sky.

"They sent his paycheck straight to his mother. Not that it was enough, not nearly. The family barely scraped by." Cook looked sharp at me, and I couldn't guess what she expected me to say.

"Can't imagine what job a boy might do in the mines," I finally ventured.

"Scraped by." Cook rolled her eyes. "Are you listening? Waste of time, thinking on the likes of Daro Michelson. Not the life you'd want."

She shooed me out, and Osten set me to waiting on one and all. I brought a lap robe up to the French lady and then shot all the way down to the other end of the house with the sandwiches for the professor. Mrs. Brookeson wanted hot tea and the chance to complain. I skirted Osten's office, as I didn't need yet another run-in with him, then took the mail, mostly magazines, over to the ladies' big basket.

To think I had worried I'd be bored! Summer had been all about catering to the masses, with a weekly dance, organized picnics or sailing for the younger set, and shopping trips, carriage rides to scenic views, and swell afternoon tea parties, card parties and piano recitals for the older.

I'd have easily believed life would become quieter, even dull, with so few guests…and yet now, with so few staff, I ran around busier than ever.

"Elizabeth, Elizabeth!" Avery, his voice little more than a croak, tried to shout.

I didn't need to see his red-rimmed eyes, or greenish pallor to know he'd been up all night.

"Bit of a party, Avery?"

"Don't be a witch. Fetch some whiskey. Hair of the

dog all I need. In the smoking room; for me and Mark both."

I toyed with offering him something nasty; 'sardines in oil' popped into mind, but he appeared in no mind to enjoy a bit of my humor. Serve him right for drinking so much.

I doubled back to the gentleman's bar and hoped there'd be an open bottle so I need not request one from the grumpy Mr. Osten. I wasn't meant to hand out the liquor, even to the owner's son.

Ariel popped out of the ladies' sitting room, pen in hand. "For Avery, I take it?"

I shrugged.

"You were so right about him. Model citizen," Ariel snapped. "I should follow you in and ask if he's drinking again at this hour."

"He's in a mood. I wouldn't trouble him right now."

"Now would be the perfect time." Ariel trailed me out of the bar. "I suspect I'd find less of the perfectly behaved gentleman and more of this privileged, smarmy rich boy I suspected all along."

I wanted to flat out agree with her. Then again, he was, in a way, my employer. I shrugged again.

"Quite tongue-tied, I see."

I probably deserved Ariel's sarcasm, yet what could I do? We were in very different positions within the household. I had grabbed up a nearly full bottle from the back of the bar. Probably more than I should bring him, but it didn't appear I had much choice. "What do you want me to say?" I asked Ariel. "I suppose there are worse things than he occasionally drinks to excess."

"Yes, like, if he gambled, say." Did she guess about the gambling, or had she been spying on him?

I very nearly shrugged again but managed not to. Instead, I spoke in the tones of a Mrs. Brookeson. "As to that, I truly cannot say."

Ariel put her hands on her hips. "Will not, you mean?"

I waved the bottle. "The master awaits. If you'll excuse me."

Avery sat hunched by a pitifully small fire in the men's smoking room. Mark, apparently unconscious, draped limply over an overstuffed chair in the corner. He persisted in being the weak-willed cousin to a rich boy. I restrained myself from snorting in disgust, remembering Cook's recommendation and the ridiculous expectation for he and I. As if I would ever consider a man like him!

Dirty glasses littered the table, and the stench of cigars filled the air.

Avery jerked his head, by which I gathered I should pour.

"Join me for a drink," he grumbled.

I felt nothing whatsoever like joining the party. "I'm afraid I've things to do."

"Oh for God's sake," he bit off, suddenly angry. "A bit of companionship, isn't that what your job is supposed to be? Sit and talk with the guests, that sort of thing? If you want to work here again next year, perhaps you should be a bit more accommodating."

I eased onto a stool well away from him. "Well. If you are going to be so charming."

He hunched his shoulders and leaned forward, clutching a tumbler of whiskey in both hands. "Where the hell were you yesterday? No damn staff left in the building."

"Beryl and I went to her aunt's. We weren't far. I didn't think you were here either."

"I went to town. Told Osten I'd get boards, to board up the windows with that big storm coming in. What do you think I was doing?"

Why hadn't Osten told me so? I wondered at the odd oversight. I mean, I had asked him directly. In fact, neither one of them had mentioned any sort of storm preparations.

"You marched out the door and left the place," Avery snapped, accusingly at me.

"I'm here now. I think everyone ate and the house survived the storm and all." I might as well have been yapping like a little dog for Avery paid no heed.

He was, as ever, all caught up in his own problems. "Damn Norris. Fellow looked a fool. Fleeced us. Took my month's allowance before midnight. Finished Mark off not long after. We were down to bartering our damn watches. Rube. Met him at the pub in Ingonish. Thought we'd spend the day relieving him of all his cash."

I tsk-tsked in a sympathetic manner. A grown man whining about losing his allowance? It would do me no good to say a word of what came to my mind.

"I want my own back!" He grabbed his tumbler and threw back a large dollop of the amber liquid. It had to burn going down for he followed it with a gasping "Ahhhh."

So he had gone off to gamble yesterday, as I had guessed. He'd certainly set off uncharacteristically early. I got up and wandered over to his coat rack and waiting table. Darn it if someone hadn't again left mail for Madame C in among the men's stuff, again.

"Leave that alone," he snapped. "I'll go through it."

"Yesterday's mail," I said. "This can go right over to the front room for the ladies."

Abruptly, he yanked my arm and jerked me back to my seat. He lofted the glass, with perhaps a teaspoon full left, and barked "for you!"

He was loud enough for anyone in the hallway to overhear. The fool! He was ruining his own chances. Ariel didn't even need her ear to the door to overhear him.

I brought a finger to my lips, to try to shush him. I have no idea why. Why should I care if he ruined his best marriage prospect? Wouldn't that suit me? I suppose there was something romantic about it all. Genevieve dead-gone on him, and Avery still taking care to put his best foot forward when it came to her. Perhaps, for her, Avery would make himself a better man?

The idea of Ariel investigating him seemed somehow cruel.

Avery took no notice of my desperate shushing motions. He slopped the couple drops at my face and spun to top up the glass again.

"Honestly, Avery!" I snapped, and mopped at my face with my sleeve. Heaven knew I didn't need to walk around stinking of booze.

"No damned appreciation for anything I do, stuck here with all these so-called friends." He glanced at the unconscious Mark, then turned back to me. "You've always been a friend, then, haven't you, our Miss

Eames? So very competent, aren't you? You'd like to do even better here, wouldn't you?"

I hardly noticed what he said. I was worried about Ariel overhearing. He reached over and placed a hand on my knee. "I need an assistant myself, don't I? A personal assistant. You could work directly for me."

"Lucky me." I scrambled back from him. "Right now, I should get back to my job here."

Avery grabbed my arm, dragged me down and whispered in my ear, "You've always been my favorite, but you know that, don't you?"

His hot, boozy breath, and heavy, lurching movement made me step back into the corner. "Excuse me."

He grasped my arm, staggered, leaned heavily on my shoulder while pressing me backward toward the long settee.

"So accommodating," he slurred.

I scuttled sideways and tried to yank my arm free.

"You still want a job, do you?"

He slammed his lips down on mine.

I fell back as he bore down, harder and harder. I squirmed sideways off the settee and out from under his hammering embrace. He hung on my arm and dragged me down. I fell to my knees to get away from him and crawled sideways, hampered by the hem of my skirt catching on something.

He gathered a bunch of sweater in his fist and yanked me back abruptly. "Whoa there, old Nellie. I'm not done with you."

I fell backward, and falling, flung my free hand out to catch myself. I hit the floor and pain shot up my arm. I shrieked as I jerked myself away and nearly crashed down onto the unforgiving bricks of the hearth. As I rolled away from him my hand landed on the poker he'd been using for the fire.

"Oh for God's sake," Avery snarled. He leaned over to grab my hand. I assume he meant to grab my hand. Oh, heaven only knew what he planned next.

I rolled back over, the fireplace poker still clutched in my hand. It slammed directly into the intersection of his trousers' inseam, the area one might indelicately call 'the crotch.' I can honestly claim it was no plan of mine, but somehow, a happy accident.

He screamed.

The hallway door slammed open and Ariel charged into the room, but froze at the madness before her.

I struggled to sit up, stuck as I was between the chair, the hassock and Avery's flailing body. Avery, still drunk I realized, flopped to the floor, clutching his crotch and groaning.

Mark snored, very gently, from the comfort of the easy chair not two steps away. We'd overturned the little side table. Candy almonds, in their pinks and pale blues, littered the floor all around us.

We all endured several seconds in silence. That is, Ariel and I remained silent, looking at the groaning and gagging man on the floor.

"I ah, er." Eventually, Avery clambered to his feet. "That is, ah Ariel, I stumbled. I mean..." He made a bold effort to stand upright and not clutch any embarrassing parts of his body.

Ariel advanced, glaring. She looked like some crazed Joan of Arc, if only she'd had a shield.

No doubt alarmed by the killer look in her eye, Avery hurriedly said, "This isn't what it looks like. I mean, Elizabeth, you tell her."

I cannot say what I might have said, or what I meant to say. I started to sit up, and reached out to place my hand on the floor. Pain shot up my arm.

To my horror, a sob burst out of me as pain overrode both fear and confusion. I clutched my wrist and tried to stifle the next sob.

"Oh, for heaven sake." Avery half turned toward me, ready to bark something, no doubt.

Ariel raised the poker I had held, like a firebrand. "Swine," she snarled. "Attacking the help? You are never ever good enough for my sister. You think I haven't been watching you? I've seen what you do. I've kept an eye on you for weeks." She started to jab and Avery actually turned and belted off into the hallway.

I scurried away as well. I ran down the hall, mindlessly clutching my arm. I burst into the kitchen like a creature quite possessed, thinking no more than to find Cook there, and... I don't even know my intentions.

In any case, Cook was not there. She'd taken her afternoon break and gone.

I thundered into the kitchen and straight into the arms of 'my Daro.'

Chapter Six
Rescue

Daro Michelson stumbled back. I looked like heaven-only-knew what.

He didn't ask or guess or try to converse. He wasn't embarrassed. I gulped back a sob and tried to about-face, stumbled, and put out a hand to catch myself.

Mr. Michelson stepped forward and caught me in his arms and swung me, ever so gently, onto a kitchen chair.

"You've been in some rough seas, Captain." He pulled out a bright red, much crumpled handkerchief. "Just the ticket." He handed it to me.

I mopped my face with it, one handed, holding my arm at an awkward angle. I felt so embarrassed.

Daro pulled a long face and said, in his same gravelly voice that sounded like it should belong to a giant, "Are you all right?"

In spite of it all, I giggled. I managed to nod my head. Then the tears started again.

Looking back, I suppose, it was all the things he didn't do that set him apart. A fellow of Avery's ilk would have been annoyed. My father would have marched off saying 'I'll called your mother.' Osten would have stood about, coughing.

Nor did Daro have the suave gift of words like our

old driver George, who'd say something like "No need to cry, beautiful girl. You know I'll do anything at all to see you smile."

No, Daro gently took hold of the arm I was cradling and murmured, "What have you done to this arm now, Captain? The wrist is swelling already." He set my wrist under running water in the sink, then helped me settle in back in the chair as he cast about for a towel. We settled for a dish towel, and rested my wrist on that.

He moved it gently. "Not broken. Still, a nasty bruise. Right along the bone. That will throb. Keep the cold on it." He eased my arm into the great basin cook used for everything. "Best to do this, off and on."

The cold took the pain, and suddenly, I felt more embarrassed than anything. "It's nothing. I'm going to make a cup of tea, Mr. Michelson. I am so sorry."

"Shh. No need, Captain. You'll tell me if you need anything, if you want me to do anything or not, won't you?" He had the deep dark soulful eyes of a hound. I knew he meant what he said. If I asked him to toss Avery out on his ear, it would take him no more than a matter of moments.

It all seemed quite ridiculous suddenly. I giggled through my tears and, feeling crazy, made an effort to pull myself together. "There is something, as a matter of fact. I'd like you to call me by name."

"Name?"

"Yes. Mine is Elizabeth. It's actually quite rare for anyone to call me 'Captain.' "

Distantly, someone started to play a Gaelic-sounding tune on the piano. Cook must be listening to George play in the dining hall. He often came in for a cup of coffee of an afternoon and was the most beautiful musician. Thank heaven for our gifted chauffer, for it meant Mrs. Buxton, at least, wasn't here to witness my hysteria.

In fact, almost no one noticed. Why, anything could be going on in a corner of this vast place, with no one the wiser. I wrapped my useless shawl tighter around me and crouched by the stove.

I should have been shattered, planning my departure, or screaming with fury. Instead, my mind kept turning back to sailing through storm on the *Thistle*. I pictured how Daro had wrapped his arms right 'round me so he could grasp the wheel next to my hands.

Thick dark hairs curled up over the edge of his shirt collar and he smelled of salty sea air.

I suppose I sat there silent, clutching my arm, for ages. He must have guessed I'd suffered more than a common household accident.

He glanced at the hallway door, turned back to me. "You want me to have a word with someone here?"

"Oh no. I'm fine." Heavens, let him not go tackle Avery. I shook my head quickly. "Silly accident. I um, I was chatting with Cook yesterday, and she said you grew up far off in Sydney."

He stepped away. "A long time ago."

"Surely, I mean, you must miss people you knew there?" I tried not to cling to his arm.

He smiled suddenly, so suddenly. "You know, I do. I never think of that part of it. I remember the mines, getting up early so I could see a few minutes of daylight, but I did like the folks. I stayed with the Stewart family, and remember the missus reading poetry in the firelight of an evening as we kids fell asleep."

"Poems." I had to smile. "You know your poetry."

He motioned for me to put my wrist back into cold water. "I still hear Tennyson as if spoken in Mrs. Stewart's voice. Those years weren't all an awful time and nice of you think of it, and to remind me."

A tap at the door announced Ariel. She stuck her head around the corner.

She and Daro looked at one another for a long moment, and then she said, in a rather low voice, "Tea?"

"Tea." I nodded, as if all were ordinary. She looked as if she had expected hysterics.

I didn't care. The scene with Avery felt as distant and unreal as if I'd watched it on stage, as if it wasn't real at all. Daro stood there, as calm as if he still faced down the monster waves in that storm.

Likely, I was about to find myself out of a job. I should have been devastated, but all I could think was I'd never see Daro again.

Ariel bustled into the massive kitchen as if she were perfectly at home there. She flipped back her luxuriant auburn locks and smoothed her hands down her long-line plaid day suit. Any man could be forgiven for giving her another look.

Daro didn't. He held my wrist in his massive paw for a moment longer. "Send word if you need me."

"Don't go on my account," Ariel said. She set out the common mugs and grabbed up the oversized tea kettle.

"Halibut waiting," he said briefly, by which I supposed he meant to go fish.

I shivered as he left, in spite of the heat emanating from the huge old black stove.

Ariel, ever practical, jumped to her feet. "Let me fetch you something. You're freezing."

I leaned over the stove, glad for a moment alone. I shut my eyes, but even with the incredible warmth washing over me, another shiver ran up my spine.

"Here, slide your arms into this." Ariel held out a soft jacket of cashmere or something equally soft and expensive, and started to ease it over my arm.

"I couldn't borrow such a lovely thing."

"Nonsense. In fact, you can have it. My mother purchased it for me and look how sallow it makes my complexion." She held a sleeve up to her face. "Hideous, isn't it? I've noticed you wear yellow nicely. Brings out the highlights in your hair. You keep it."

I pulled off my own too-thin, shawl—one of those 'height of fashion but useless' creations, and slid my arm into the exquisite, soft silk lining of her jacket. "I love it." I started to hang my shawl over the back of a chair, then thought better of it. "You know what? This shawl was from my Mum. I had asked for some warm things from home. You have it."

"Really?" Ariel looked startled. "Why, you know, I've quite admired the elaborate stitch-work. I suppose it isn't exactly practical, is it?"

At exactly the same moment, we both said, "Mothers," and giggled. We might have always been friends.

"Ariel, why did you suspect Avery might do something nasty? If you hadn't charged in, I don't want to imagine what might have happened."

She plopped down on the stool by the warming

oven. "Siobhan Bryant."

"Siobhan? The lovely housemaid with the long dark hair?"

Ariel nodded. "She left early in the season and abruptly. Made me wonder, that's all. I overheard Avery growl something about her to Osten weeks ago, and it's not like he could have meant someone else, could he? Her first name is so uncommon. So, I listened in. Avery told Osten to send her money."

We looked at each other, undoubtedly thinking precisely the same thing. A pretty girl, sent home for no apparent reason? I finally made myself say, "It might mean…something else."

"It might, but why other than having been too familiar, would Avery send a maid money? I don't claim to know for certain, but it was overhearing about her that made me start checking up on Avery." She leaned back in the old kitchen chair and mused, "I realized that we actually knew very little about him."

I guess I looked horrified.

"I still don't know about Siobhan for sure, mind you. A miserable way to treat a girl, and to send a young girl home, even with some cash, in that condition."

"If it's true."

"Likely is. I'm surprised we haven't had her father or someone here kicking up a fuss." She looked straight at me. "Gambling, boozing. Avery's behavior with you. I guess I've seen enough. I don't know what I am going to do next, but I have to do something."

"Do?"

Ariel leaned across the great stone counter as she said, "My sister Genevieve is a sweet, sweet person.

She adores him. I can't exactly tell her he's a cad. She won't want to believe it. We must break it up. You will help me, won't you Elizabeth? You aren't fooled by him. I have to do something soon."

"I can't see how I can help." I busied myself with the tea tray, unaccountably anxious about what she might stir up.

"We can tell Avery we know all about Siobhan. We'll threaten to ruin him in society." Ariel crossed her arms with finality.

"We don't know if it's true." I kept my gaze fixed upon the pattern on the teapot.

"If the threat scares him, we'll know it is true," she insisted. "He's to break it off with Gen. He can tell her how he has suddenly fallen for someone else. Whatever."

"He won't tell Gen anything of the kind," I protested. "He's been trying to impress her since back in the summer."

"Yes. Quite suddenly, he became quite attentive, didn't he? His mother became positively friendly, too." She leaned back, hands on hips. "As they both seemed disinclined to begin with, it makes me suspicious."

"Everything makes you suspicious, Ariel." I felt I had to point out. "But, if he actually likes her, he might admit more than you would want, when he breaks it off. Admit we are forcing him."

"Then he can just go. I'll tell her that he left. He won't want to be ruined in society." She shrugged. "Why are you arguing? If he stays, he's going to make sure you are dismissed. I mean, for you it's only a job, but for Gen this matters."

A job might seem like a minor thing to Ariel, with

who knew what inheritance, but it was no small matter for me. I'd have to go home and take up the roll of a wallflower again. My fingers clenched at the thought. All those town ladies with nothing to do but gossip. My mum was no better than any of her neighbors, either. She'd love to have both daughters married to men that let her gloat. Oh, I did not want to return home.

I'd not seen Daro again.

My heart skipped a beat at the thought. Even after all of it; the storm and the danger and unpleasantness, I hated the idea of leaving Cape Breton Island: Cape Breton, and the one man who was most definitely 'better.'

Ariel set off, determined. As for me; I could only await my fate.

Chapter Seven
McClellan Harbor

No deliveries were expected on Tuesday and I sadly poked around in the chilly front rooms. A fine dusting of snow had settled over the porch, the road, and a thicker line of snow sat out along the high-tide mark on the beach. It looked as if winter had arrived overnight.

It felt like the end. I had reached the end of my time in this, the most beautiful place on earth, and an end to seeing Daro.

My Daro.

Silly. I tried to dismiss the thought. I couldn't allow myself these foolish notions. For one thing, my parents' views would only echo Cook's. For another, the man himself was hardly beating a path to the door, was he? I had drummed up this great affection out of nothing. I had to stop kidding myself.

I wound the grandfather clock in the hallway. The heavy tick-tock swelled to fill the silence. I stood there in the emptiness. I could see no way to avoid departure.

I waited to hear Avery's footsteps on the front stairs. Immediate dismissal seemed likely, given yesterday's events. In fact, I anticipated a nasty scene. I should have packed before I came downstairs. Even if I could somehow smooth things over, the hotel was obviously not prepared for winter. Oceanside's days had to be numbered, regardless.

I tugged my sweater down over my arms as a draft worked its way through the gaps in the wood over the front windows. No one had ordered replacement windows yet. The boards were unsightly and the draft made the room cold. Proper wool drapes would make the world of difference.

Ariel had mentioned the seamstress in McLellan's Harbor.

Drapes! Yes, in fact, why not? I was still employed, at least, for the moment. I could go out on an errand to order drapes. I might find this seamstress lady in the village where Daro's family lived. Perhaps I would run into Daro?

I so wanted the chance for some final word.

I estimated measurements by eye and slid the pretty, butter-soft cashmere from Ariel over my best everyday dress, took some time get my hair perfect and set off pretending I was on an ordinary errand. I wasted no time cadging a ride in George's lovely automobile to the village at McLellan's harbor. I could hardly suppose the seamstress' shop would be open this early, but I could wait. I would dawdle about the little town and see who I happened into.

Fog stretched in layers above the sea, sank into troughs between waves, and wove in and out through the rocks near shore. The red dawn of the morning sky had not yet completely faded.

George dropped me at the base of the hill. "I'm due back at Oceanside to pick up Mrs. Brookeson after breakfast time." George rolled his eyes. "The complaints I get, if I am one minute late."

"Not to worry, I can find my way from here," I said

as I set off up the narrow lane. McLellan's was not particularly familiar, though I'd traveled through a few times. It sprang up, like many a seaside village, overlooking a useful, mostly natural harbor.

Small, much-weathered homes crowded up the side of a hill. All their front windows looked out over the sea. Their lighthouse sat on a curving point of rock, and fishing boats dotted the waters. Men were busy about the docks, but few other people were about in the fresh, cold morning.

Southward, a plump cloud bank sank down and squashed into the horizon. Our hotel artist would have set up canvas right there, had he one look at the scene; he often talked about 'capturing the atmosphere.'

I would paint the village if I had the skill of an artist. Never mind the curling waves or dramatic clouds stretched across the opalescent sky. I'd paint this first cottage, with its beach roses all faded and dusted with snow. I'd catch the arched doorway of the next house, made from the hull of a rowboat. I would somehow share the charm.

I meandered up the lane, peering into people's snowy front gardens and wondering about their lives here. I quite forgot to keep an eye out for the seamstress. A twist in the lane led me up a slight rise and I walked around a corner practically right into my Daro. Mr. Michelson. He was stacking crates onto a wagon.

I stumbled to a stop and felt my cheeks flush with embarrassment. All good and well to imagine 'happening' into him, quite another to do it! If he hadn't already seen me, I think I might have turned and run. This visit could never be mistaken for happenstance.

"Captain." He straightened up slowly. The array of wooden boxes attested to how early he set into his workday. It was surely still early and he looked at me curiously.

"I'm running some errands, Mr. Michelson," I said hastily. I wished I had something in my hands—curtains to repair, anything to give some evidence of my errand.

He grinned. "Have they sent you after fish this morning?"

"Drapes," I said. "I'm to order drapes."

Daro abruptly set aside the box in his hands. "Drapes?"

"Yes. Heavy wool drapes."

"They can't be thinking of staying longer? Drapes now." His deep, rumbling voice might have come from the depths of the ocean, and indeed, all I could think of was how he had stood by me, so sure, aboard the *Thistle*. He frowned as he stared to the south. "It was intended as a summer place. They never intended to heat it! I'll speak to one of the town fathers. Someone must convince the Brookesons of the danger. The hotel was never meant to house folks all winter. It will likely be cut off…"

He paused just then, and, not quite looking at me, said, "You'll not be going yourself, I mean, not 'til they close?"

"I hope to stay." As I spoke I realized my comment must seem terribly forward! "Until close, I mean."

Daro reached out to grasp my hand, hesitated. "Wrist?"

"It's okay."

He grasped my fingers as if I were as delicate as a doll.

I held perfectly still.

We stood hand-in-hand, not quite looking at one another. My heart was racing and my mouth was so ridiculously dry, I couldn't utter a word.

We remained right there, hand-in-hand, in the middle of this little lane, in front of any who cared to look, for what length of time I could scarcely say. I can only guess he felt as surprised as I.

"Seamstress, then?" Daro suddenly asked.

With particularly brilliant eloquence, I nodded.

Daro started to turn and point, as I tucked my hand around his elbow, thinking he meant to escort me. He paused. Realizing my mistake, I started to step away. We were completely at cross-purposes, but he stepped off and placed a hand over mine, as if he'd intended to walk with me from the first.

We were both blushing madly. Quite madly! Oh, my goodness, I wanted to laugh but wished he would, before I.

He paced off down the lane quietly though. "If only winter weren't so close," he said at last.

With my hand tucked in his arm, I scarcely heard him. I am not at all sure my feet touched the ground. The perfect pearly clouds above took on the shape of swans adrift and the surf might have been music.

"Drapes now," he muttered.

I managed to pull myself together. "The house feels chilly, but Mr. Osten has ordered another lot of firewood and I'm sure we can make the front rooms snug."

"It isn't full winter yet."

We arrived at a small wooden sign for Eleanor Dobbs Fine Stitchery. No tracks lead up the dressmaker's front walk. It was really too early to call. Few tracks marked even the main road. Fewer yet were the tracks along this lane. I stopped short and gazed at her still-shaded windows.

I regretted the end of our walk, though Daro made no move to step away. I kept my hand tucked in at his elbow.

"It won't be snug," he growled, returning to his concern about Oceanside. "It won't be safe."

Oceanside, enchantingly, had been built right on the beach itself. Yet, compared to the many tiny homes here, it seemed utterly impervious to weather. Oh, we might suffer the odd broken window, but what more could possibly trouble the great building?

"This whole village lives here all winter long," I pointed out.

A red-trimmed punt wallowed in waves not three meters off from the dock at the lighthouse. A fellow in a knit hat bent over the stern, dipping his hands in the freezing cold Atlantic. It might as easily have been Daro out there, hauling nets.

"Look at the bluff and at the rocks and the shape of the barrier shoals," Daro pointed. "Look. The land here protects the village. The old folks knew what they were about when they first built their homes here. On the other hand, those clever fellows from away south set Oceanside right on an open beach at a particularly low point. It's lovely in summer. Winter is another story. In bad storms, we've seen waves come right up over the road along there. Oceanside might have more than broken windows, next time."

I looked up and down the village streets, which all lined the hillside, with the protection of the natural breakwater before them.

"The cold presents a challenge," he continued. "The builders should have known what they were doing, but for some reason, built the whole place as inexpensively as possible. Sure it looks grand."

Grand? Oceanside looked enormous. I could hardly point out how frail all these little box houses appeared by comparison. It didn't seem polite. I felt perfectly confident in the great structure, even if I had less confidence in its inhabitants.

"Real waves. I'm not talking about the bit of spray like last time," Daro said. "Waves could roll right up on that fancy house's porch. And, the place would crumble."

I watched the glitter of the Sun reflecting on the waves in front of me. Oceanside seemed far, far away. "If braving winter storms is the only way for me to stay, why then." I shrugged.

"I'll see you out in plenty of time, if there's any danger," Daro said. "I can always see weather coming in."

My heart leapt. If I had my wits about me, I might have said something romantic. I should have murmured a sweet little 'I'll trust you to save me, Daro.' Instead, I stood and gawked up at him, in a completely besotted fashion. He likely found me impossibly silly.

He smiled back down at me, a tremendous, good-hearted bear of a man.

So we stood, not speaking, not knowing what more to say, or what more we should say, and unmindful of the village waking around us. We both clung to this as a most precious moment. At least, I assumed he was speechless for the same reason as I.

Eventually, doors slammed and it occurred to me that people might be looking. I pulled myself together. "Do show me around the village?"

Daro raised his eyebrows, but nodded, and we set off. Then I remembered about the seamstress, as we strolled away from her door! Oh, well. He'd already seen through my little subterfuge, without a doubt.

We went down the long lane and along the waterfront. Daro gazed intently southward again. The wind swirled the fog into elaborate patterns up from the breakers, over the jagged line of granite and up almost to our feet.

I felt plenty warm enough, though the wind off the sea brought a shower of fine freezing droplets mixed with snowflakes. We puttered along the village road, under the clock sign where we were better protected from the sea spray.

"My friend Ariel is dead-set on breaking up her sister and Avery Brookeson," I said, mostly for conversation.

"Bit heartless?"

"She means well," I tried to explain. "Avery and Gen. I don't know what to say. Gen; she's a lovely, friendly person but gullible. You know what I mean? Ariel, the sister, so wants Gen to meet someone pleasant, someone kind."

"Isn't that what anyone would want?"

"Yes, yes, I suppose so." I felt I explained it all poorly. Avery no more cared for Gen than he did about old *Thistle;* great to show off and worth a good bit of dough, but when it came to it, replaceable.

Gen most certainly came with 'a good bit of dough.' Their marriage would be a disaster though. I could see, as Ariel so plainly could, down the road to a time when Gen would be at best ignored or made miserable, while Avery went on with the lifestyle of a rake. She was a patriot, too, and had no grasp of how Avery belittled his home country.

I was hard pressed to explain why I even cared. A society gal marrying someone in her own class and the two making such a lovely couple, wouldn't it be what they both deserved?

"You're better off out of it," Daro advised.

"I am out of it, or will be, soon," I admitted. Likely, I'd be fired the moment Avery saw me. I recalled how this was likely my last chance, my last visit with Daro. I suppose I held his hand all the tighter as we went. I wondered if it would be ridiculous to promise to write, after so brief an acquaintance.

I puzzled over the finer points of such etiquette as we came by the very recognizable Trumbull house. The dusting of snow sat particularly elegantly there, with ice crystals dangling from the picket fence and all along the edges of the famous Trumbull widow's walk.

The widow Trumbull herself shuffled down her walk and stood stock-still at her gate.

"Morning, Mrs. Trumbull," Daro said.

"Daro Michelson," she said, in her best, retired-now schoolmarm manner. I could see her in front of a classroom easy as pie. She'd probably been Daro's schoolmarm, those short years he'd spent in a classroom.

"Do you need something, Mrs. Trumbull?"

She pulled a scarf around tighter against the biting

wind. "Look what's happened to my lantern." She nodded to the high lantern on the post at the end of her walk. Several of the small square panes in the shaped lantern were gone. They were not smashed. They were simply missing.

Daro frowned as he studied it and the snow around the base. At length, he picked a shard of glass from the back panel. "This pane was broken, but the glass chimney inside for the flame is gone. That didn't break." He stood on tiptoe to peer into the inner workings. "The entire oil reservoir is gone, jar and all. Pried right out of there."

"I lit the candle last evening. Perfectly usual." Mrs. Trumbull twisted a handkerchief about in her hands. Since her husband was lost at sea half-a-century ago Mrs. Trumbull had, rather famously, kept her home alight. Lights atop the widow's walk shone at any hour, and her front lantern burned from sundown to sun up, without fail.

"It can't have broken? We've had some fierce wind gusts."

Daro shook his head, still looking around the yard. "There are indents here, not-quite covered tracks." His gaze followed the unclear marks in her front garden.

"I came down just now, to douse the light."

"There are faint tracks right up your porch steps."

The woman motioned toward the porch. "I keep a big jar of oil right back of the column post there."

We all trudged up the stairs to look. Sure enough, the spare oil jar was also gone.

"Who would do such a thing? They ruined the lamp, besides." The woman stood shivering in her indoor-shawl, staring about the porch as if this missing glass jar might suddenly emerge.

"I'm sure we can fix the lantern," I said. "Hadn't you better go inside? It is so cold."

The incredibly dignified woman straightened and looked me up and down as if I had only then leapt up out of a hole in the ground. "You're from this new resort?"

"Yes."

She looked rather pointedly back at Daro.

I could read her, plain as plain. I folded my hands together and said, "I'm staff."

"From away." She sniffed. She could take up where Cook's comments left off, easily enough. Even If I wasn't as inappropriate as 'a society gal,' still, I did not belong with the likes of Daro.

As if it were any of her business. I wanted to dismiss her straightaway. Yet, did I do much the same sort of thing, judging Avery and Gen?

I turned to look out over the sea and clasped my hands behind my back. Avery and Gen were not the same thing at all, I decided. My judgment came from knowing the two of them, not simply because of their circumstances.

Daro hadn't heard us or didn't understand. He fussed with remnants of the light, offered to go after parts for a repair, and began measuring for replacement panes. He didn't notice my discomfort. Perhaps he thought it didn't matter. Perhaps he didn't care.

I hated to admit it, but feared I would meet Mrs. Trumbull's sort of short-sighted disapproval over and over again. Her way of thinking was hardly outdated. I decided I would not let her ruin my day. Nothing mattered but the two of us and soon I would again be arm-in-arm with the man I…oh dear heavens. What was I letting myself believe?

My heart sank. I hadn't given a thought to other people, had I? What folks would say, or for that matter, what my parents would say. Oh, better not even to think of them. I knew what they intended. They had planned for me to take up with a man like Avery. Or Mark. Yes, he did seem more and more like Mum's choice, all along.

Why, if my sister were here, she'd be as dedicated as Ariel, hell-bent on breaking up her sister's pursuit of this local fisherman.

Of course, the entire affair might be in my imagination. Daro had not come calling for me, had he? What if he was merely being kind? Why, he'd not said one word, had he? He'd never said anything to imply his admiration. Oh, it was all good and well for me to relive those moments when we walked hand-in-hand through the most magical fog, but here, in the full light of day, things appeared different.

I suppose I looked grim, thinking such thoughts. Suddenly the old lady leaned forward and whispered low, "It's a hard thing not to be part of things. To come from away and never quite fit-in." She pressed my hand tightly.

Much as I didn't care to, I understood. Her voice gave away. She was, herself 'from away.' She might have married in, she might be respected, but did she get invites to the odd family musical events the locals so loved? Did people drop by for a cup of coffee? Did George come by and offer to play the piano? The Doughty's lived a mile up the road, but had Mrs. Trumbull ever heard Donnall's 'beautiful voice?' I suspected not. She was quietly alone, too dignified to admit to being lonely.

I thought of her long years in this great old Victorian house, probably built with the idea of having several children, but then waiting all these years for a man who had likely died half a century ago. I shivered.

"I've a shawl I can lend you," Mrs. Trumbull immediately offered. I felt the worse, for thinking badly of her at first.

"I'd be most appreciative," I said, mostly because I wanted to accept her kind gesture. I followed her in to her front foyer. It felt as large and grand as Oceanside itself, though it echoed with emptiness.

Daro thumped in after us, looked at the lock on the door and nodded briskly. "I'll stop by with something to get a light going out front again, Mrs. Trumbull. I'm glad to see they didn't attempt to get in the house."

As we left, I realized I wanted to stay. I wished to explore the fabulous house. I would love to see a portrait of the Captain, her husband. Oh, what a romance it must have been, to keep her here waiting and hoping all these years! Everyone knew how she had waited with endless hope and loyalty, a young bride left all alone here, presumed a widow.

As I wrapped myself in her mint-green hand-knit shawl, I imagined the rest of the house; a dining room to rival the great hall at Oceanside, a sitting room with a tea set from the Far East, and somewhere, an elegant portrait of her husband, the sea caption.

I mused silently as we strolled along.

Daro seemed rather quiet, too. He walked us along the point, to the foot of the lighthouse. He pointed south toward the rocky shoreline, where I'd very nearly crashed the *Thistle*. "A strange false light from a fire. Then, lamp oil and a lantern's mirror are stolen. We can see it now."

"We can?"

"You can send out a more-sure, steady light with the mirror and a proper big lamp, than from a bonfire on the beach, can't you now?"

"Mm." I didn't care about the lantern. Had he worried what his family would say about me? Had he given us any thought at all? They probably already had some nice village girl all picked out for him, or some lass from Ingonish, who'd fit in nicely with the family.

Daro crossed his arms and looked thoughtfully at the sea. "We sailed up past this point ourselves. We saw Mrs. Trumbull's."

"Yes," I agreed. "It was recognizing Mrs. Trumbull's that saved us."

"The answer is obvious. Someone's going to try wrecking." He glared at the moderate waves, glittering in the morning light. "They tried trickery with a bonfire. They nearly fooled the two of us, didn't they? But looking back, the light we saw flickered, didn't it? With a proper lantern and mirror, they can make their false look more like a proper, steady lighthouse beacon. If they can trick a ship into taking it for a navigational light, they could lure one into the shallows."

"Fool ships?" I didn't grasp what he was talking so urgently about, nor much care. We'd gone up and down the lane. I probably ought to take my leave and go to the seamstress' shop. I'd planned to ask him to write when I set out this morning, hadn't I? I must at least ask.

"Wrecking. Some ships carry a fortune in goods."

"I came today, to ask, I mean, to leave my address," I forced myself to say.

Daro's mind was far off, in the tumbling waves rolling so relentlessly to shore. "They lure a ship in too close to shore, so it crashes into rocks or a beach, and then they salvage whatever washes up. They grab as much cargo as they can, with never a care for lives lost in the process."

Sea fog swamped the road south of us, leading to the resort. All tire tracks disappeared into the soupy fog, not many paces from us. Oddly, more than the tracks from George's automobile marked the road. I let go of Daro to stroll down a little way. Clear tracks marked the lane south. The little intersection was crisscrossed with tracks, of two different sizes.

"It's an old, old crime."

"Who would have been up and out so early today?" I looked down at the tracks. "This driver might have seen someone break Mrs. Trumbull's lantern."

"Or been the one to break it," grumbled Daro.

Avery popped into my mind. The hotel's large open-topped touring car was the only other automobile in the area. Why would Avery visit this little fishing village, though? And so early. It made no sense.

Daro ambled over and looked up and down. "George must have dropped you off then gone straight back south. He would have noticed someone else driving by."

"I'll ask George when he picks me up. I wonder if Avery drove through quite early this morning."

"Avery is the son of the owners? Thinks himself the boss? Tell me something Elizabeth." Daro looked pointedly at my wrist. "What happened yesterday? Was it him?"

"Yesterday was nothing," I said quickly. "Just our Ariel, one of our guests, stirring up things. She's er...determined to break up her sister Gen and Avery." Hastily, I went on to say, "I must try to remember to ask George about this morning."

Daro shook his head. "You forget, oh Captain, exactly who has paid George to do all these errands and trundle all the staff from the hotel around all summer. George is nobody's fool. He'll not have a job if he talks about his boss's business, will he?"

"True." I admitted. Still, it was a puzzle. Mrs. Trumbull's lantern mechanism and oil taken, and an automobile had plainly visited this morning, before dawn.

I reminded myself of my real purpose here and steeled myself to try again. I might well be leaving and I wanted to give him my home address. Home address, home address chimed insanely in my head. How forward, how ridiculous. He'd never given me the slightest reason to suppose...to suppose anything! Still, I couldn't simply leave. I had to somehow speak. It might be my only chance.

"I'm likely to be packing," I squeaked.

"Be ready." He nodded briskly. "Best course. We could have a big storm any minute. They should have closed long since."

I could hardly explain it would just be me leaving; fired the moment I set foot across the threshold. I'd hoped for some plan for the future, but I could hardly insist that he accept my parents' address, could I? It was beyond me to leap beyond the etiquette. Finally, sadly, I murmured, "I'll miss you."

Chapter Eight
Ariel's Success

Ariel came into brunch alongside the French lady. I arrived at almost the same moment.

The old art professor, already waiting, had angled his chair so he could enjoy the sunlight coming through the east-side windows. "The atmospheric effects with light here are always interesting," he enthused. "Each day a new discovery."

The French lady shot him a withering look, pawed through the mail piled on the sideboard, glared with disgust at poor little Beryl shuffling in with a tray of fried herring, and marched off to the drawing room.

I had avoided everyone thus far. I had ordered the drapes, returned, and busied myself in the kitchen. I'd not run into Avery or even Mr. Osten. Mrs. Brookeson had thankfully departed for an early breakfast in town. I couldn't avoid them all forever, though.

As I poured coffee, I steeled myself for a final confrontation: Avery would likely march through the door next.

Instead, Ariel tiptoed over beside me. "Avery's left."

I gaped at her. "Left?"

"Last night. Gone and not coming back. I insisted."

I could hardly grasp her words. "Gone?" Avery gone and apparently without a complaint about me to the manager? A reprieve? I sank into the nearest chair. "Why? I mean, how?"

"What I told you. I insisted," Ariel whispered again. "I said I would tell the world about him and the young maid and ruin him in all good society unless he made himself scarce and gave me a few days to get Genevieve out of here." She rolled her eyes.

"You don't know if all that about the maid is true!"

She shrugged. "It must have been or he wouldn't have left, would he?"

"Whatever did your sister say?"

"I've not told Gen. Couldn't decide what to say."

"Perhaps, as he's left, she'll assume he's disinterested?" I clasped my head in my hands. Genevieve, simply give up? It seemed a forlorn hope.

"That's the idea." Ariel lowered her voice further. "At first, I thought I would try to convince her that he would fail to meet our parents' approval." She cut off quickly as the hallway door opened.

Manager Osten held the door and stepped aside to usher in Mark DeLaMore. Mark did not look around the room for Avery, as was his custom. He carefully made no eye contact with Ariel or me, either. Certainly, he knew something about the events of the previous day.

Osten addressed the ladies in the room with a half-bow, and Mark troubled about such etiquette not at all. He kept well away from both eggs and fish and instead, set about straining a fresh cup of coffee through the press.

Genevieve giggled her way into the room, paused at the head of the table, glanced all around and pouted. One might have imagined the dashing Avery had a habit of waiting for her every morning.

"Oh dear, has Avery already gone out this morning?" She looked expectantly at the side door. My heart sank. She was so lovely and had plainly taken such pains, even though her best efforts usually went slightly awry. She had on a smart tailored morning dress and she'd added a shimmery scarf of purple, and somewhat less wonderfully, a bright yellow narrow scarf above that. Obviously, Ariel hadn't dawdled upstairs to coax her sister into wearing a more conventional array of colors.

She asked again, "Avery?"

Poor Gen. What a nasty way for a relationship to end, with him abruptly departing. I felt so badly for her.

"Gone and gone," snarled Mark.

"Oh? An early riser for once? Do tell me, did he discover his almonds yesterday? Did he guess who left them?" She clapped her hands, gleeful.

Mark swung around sharp enough for the coffee to slop from his cup. "He has quit this place entirely. Very likely caught the early ferry this morning." He glared at Ariel and muttered again, "Gone."

"Gone," Genevieve repeated, frozen, her hand at her throat. "Was he called away?" Her snow-white face looked suddenly ashen, her soft eyes, disbelieving.

Ariel scrambled to her feet. "Genevieve?"

Her sister did not glance at her, but stared at Mark. "He surely left me some word? I mean, some explanation surely, for all of us, all his friends here?"

"He said he had enough of Cape Breton Island. He has no plans to return." How Mark could turn, so unfeeling, from the beautiful girl in front of him, I could not understand. How would one not reach out a hand, or say some word of comfort?

Ariel grabbed her arm and steered her to a chair.

"Oh, surely, Avery must have said something? There will be a card?" Genevieve grasped her sister's hand. "Do you know what is going on?"

The two of them had become, in some macabre fashion, the focus of attention in the little hall. Our manager, the artist, and even Beryl all watched surreptitiously from their various corners.

All unplanned, I bounded to my feet. "Let me pour you fresh coffee, Professor? Beryl, hadn't you better get back in there and start clearing up the kitchen?"

Osten, for all he looked like an aging ferret, was not completely insensible either. He strolled out across the hallway and began the thankless and near pointless task of chatting with the French lady.

Genevieve carried on as if unaware she might be the center of attention. "Of course, he's never said anything. Not formally, I mean. He's been most correct, a darling, all summer. Every minute coming up with some entertainment or chatting about the news, or talking about shows and things we'd see this winter, in the city."

Ariel patted her sister's hand and looked, most despairingly, at me.

"Why I assumed, of course, just a matter of time. Surely, there is some mistake? I should likely expect word, hadn't I? Of course, I'm disappointed he's gone, but I think he is most important to his father's business. That must be it. All the young men here have commitments, I think. I can't think why he didn't say so." Genevieve looked dreadfully pale. "He must plan on returning soon?"

Ariel kicked me ankle. What on Earth could I say?

Mark had said his piece, giving the idea that Avery had dumped her. Dumped her without a word. Now I was supposed to say that too? It might be in her best interest, but seemed cruel to me. She plainly adored him.

I folded my hands in front of me. "He did not leave any word with me."

"I'll speak to his mother?" Genevieve still held a hand at her throat. "I expect he'll be back shortly. It must all be a mistake."

Ariel glared at me.

Very quickly, I said, "He did not mention returning. I expect Oceanside must close soon, anyhow."

A faint rustle in the room alerted me that not only did other' ears listen, but reacted to the idea of closing. Why? It made no sense. No one at the hotel had a good reason to remain, and not one among them did not have some other place to go.

Ariel stood. "I think we should prepare to depart. You know what they are saying, now storm season is upon us. The locals say this place should be closed up and boarded."

"Depart? But his mother says she will not." Genevieve stood. "Truly, he's left with no word at all? Do you mean to tell me that this, is it? He means his departure to tell me how he feels? Or perhaps, does not feel?" Her voice broke on the last bit, yet, she still stood there, courageously, letting all of us see her heartbreak.

I found I could not utter a word. It was all so horrible and tragic and painfully public. I wanted to scream out the truth. Ariel had contrived all this, with her threat to disgrace him. I wasn't even convinced our suspicions about Siobhan had any truth to them, although why would he go, if they didn't? Oh, it was all too complex to understand.

"He's left me," Genevieve repeated.

Ariel seized her moment. "I'm afraid that is what he meant."

Genevieve spun and ran from the room. Ariel rushed after her.

****

I gladly volunteered to accompany our French lady to Ingonish town, as an escape from the unpleasantness.

Ainsley-mare obliged most willingly. The great Clydesdale met me at the gate, ears pricked, happy for the attention. I thanked my stars the hotel had thought to keep a horse on hand, for I could have never managed the newfangled automobile contraption on my own. As it was, I was doubtful about maneuvering the sleigh. The grand resort could not have up an ordinary sleigh, but a great four-seater, with high lamps, decorative curls and elaborate carvings. It seemed enormous.

Ainslee backed cheerfully between the shafts while Madame Chatillon stood impatiently by the gate. I clucked softly and the mare walked up to the walkway and stopped politely for passengers to board. The lady took two steps and ensconced herself on the rear seat. She nodded brusquely.

I had to suppress a giggle. Chauffer now! You'd think I was a complete stranger, sitting there at the reins. I clucked and the mare moved off.

The frosty air still glittered with cold and my heart lifted as the great horse sailed forward into a trot. The snow muffled her hoof beats and the air felt fine. The few miles south to Ingonish passed as if the sleigh rode on air.

Heavy, gray-white clouds filled the southerly sky, and a shimmer of light reflected almost magically off of them. Indeed, the world became a wonder the very moment I discovered I didn't have to leave this beautiful place…or Daro. At least, not yet.

The mood changed abruptly when I pulled Ainslee up at the pub's handy hitching post.

Madame Chatillon leaned forward to address me. "I must speak to the postmistress. This, the post office station in Ingonish, or perhaps the provincial post, has mislaid letters. It is most serious. Most serious."

I had a feeling that in Paris, such failures were never tolerated. I waited for her to tell me so, but she sat, waiting for some sort of answer.

"Er. Did you want me to show you the way to the post office?"

"Thank you."

I caught our reflections in the high glass windows of the Imperial Drug Company's store. She stalked determinedly passed as I, like a little church mouse, scurried in her wake. Oh, it took no effort to imagine Madame Chatillon shrieking in her peculiar accent at the poor postmistress.

I did not want to be seen with her. As we arrived at the front door I carried straight on. "Errand," I sang out, "Be right back." I ducked off around the corner onto the narrow dirt way overlooking the town wharf and hid (yes, shamelessly hid) behind boxes lined up for shipment. Scraps of fog still hung about the waterfront, helping me hide. I tried to stand there casually, while keeping an eye out for when she might pop out of the post's building.

The back door of the fisherman's shed slammed shut and I scooted around the boxes to stay out of sight.

"Surprised you haven't gone off Sydney to work the winter." A gruff old fisherman stomped by, calling to someone out on the wharf.

"Enough work here," responded a voice I knew. It was Daro himself, down on the dock. He must have come straight down to work after I'd departed. I peeked around the piled boxes.

He stood barely meters away! I heard the thump of boxes as the men set about loading or unloading, and here I hid! Great stars and garters! I practically shrank down into a ball at the thought of being found there. How stupidly embarrassing.

I peeked very carefully around the side. Daro, poised down on the floating dock, tossed a box easily over to a man on the deck of a boat.

An older man, a grizzled graybeard, stood on the dock waving a newspaper. "Trenches. They are fighting from trenches in the dirt. Practically living down in these holes in the ground."

A dockworker shook his head at the old fellow. "Europe sounds like hell."

How did I ever land myself in such a ridiculous position? I didn't mean to overhear but didn't want to dart away quite yet, either. Thank heaven I'd changed into a dark everyday overcoat that helped me blend! My bright earlier colors would have been noticed—what with my frills and froth fluffily dancing around the edges of the stacked boxes.

Two younger fellows caught boxes from Daro and stacked them. The pair had to step lively to keep up with him. I felt lucky kept his attention entirely focused on loading the boat.

"Shooting from the air, besides. Using aero planes now. There's talk about some German pilots. What they call these fighting aces." The man shook his head again.

The older man shrugged heavily. "Never heard of such a thing."

One of the youngsters called out, "Is there ought about the British infantry and any of our boys' regiments?"

"It'll be the boats, the trans-Atlantic freighters decides it all," growled the older dockworker. "If we can't get munitions through, it won't matter who's standing on what line. It'll come down to which side controls the shipping lanes. Anyone work on the wharfs'ud know that." He bent and casually flipped a box at Daro. "Not that you'd know a thing about the sea. You'd be telling'em all about mines or how steel makes all the difference."

"All far from here," the younger fellow interceded. "No sense our arguing."

"We're told to keep an eye out. Heard St. John's fellas have spotted ships, away to the east. Paper said there'd be refugees too."

"We've heard it all before, Donnall. Ships, what kind of ships?"

"The coast guard should-a been on watch long since," Donnall replied. "Battleships might head this way. Think of all our ships carrying munitions to Britain. Those are bound to attract enemy attention."

I wondered at that these fellows' interest. We were so far from it all. At home, the local Ladies Aid Society of Halifax organized various drives, from 'warm socks for soldiers,' to promoting soirees and social events, like art gallery exhibits to help fund Red Cross efforts. It sounded all very well. Older ladies, sitting home anyway, now set to knitting with a purpose. Gentlemen at parties shouted loudly against conscription of our boys into the service (or for, depending.) I suspected their arguments made as little difference as the benefit dances.

Oh, I suppose someone made good use of the socks, somewhere. Still, events were always 'over there.' Why, all summer long I regularly served tins of imported caviar to people who were reading newspapers with headlines about food and fuel in short supply, and this being Britain's hour of need.

"Another message from our Prime Minister." The eldest fisherman on the shook out the paper and held it so the other men could see. "Warnings about railways, harbors, and ports now."

"Watching all methods of transport," Don grunted.

Daro nodded. "They are worried about German sympathizers in this country, if they are watching bridges and such."

It was common knowledge that Canada's factories churned out artillery ammunition, packed it onto railways, and sent it overland to every major port. Massive sea freighters, now with armed escort, brought the ammunition overseas.

Daro crouched lower on his stack of boxes and said, "Heard of reports of warships firing on fishing vessels as well as ammunitions freighters."

"Overseas," the young fellow said. "Not in our waters. All far from here."

"Heard some funny sightings up around Saint Paul

Island," Don said.

Another man made shushing motions. "Not the sort of thing we want to be talking about on the docks. We don't know everyone here well, do we?" He looked at Daro.

At Daro? I squinted between the boxes, but my Daro did not react. He casually kept chucking boxes.

"I guess I know everyone here as well as I know anyone." Donnall grinned at Daro. "At least I can identify a fellow I went to school with, even if he worked in Sydney for a few years!"

The older man growled, "been away," and turned to spit into the sea.

Daro looked grim. "Can't say as I wasn't."

"All them kind-a problems are in Europe," the youngster put in.

"For now," the box stacker growled. "Don't help those who have been sent over there."

"Trust in Our Father," one among them murmured. Daro bowed his head. Several quietly spoke names, probably of relatives, "Bless our Ben, keep Nicky, Old George's boy," or "Bring that fool Kyle back to us, I've not laughed since he went…" and other remembrances.

I had to pull back tears at their simple prayer. Loads of folk hereabouts, especially the fishing families, had kin on the other side of the strait. The Newfoundland boys were a loss that must have struck them all in the heart.

"You've heard from your young brother, have you now, Michelson?"

I held my breath. His brother was over there?

All this talk of war, of battles and strategies; How easy it was to forget we were talking about ordinary folks, young men from down the street or two towns over, someone's cousin, brother, or son.

"Not for weeks." Daro's gravelly voice sounded lower than ever.

His brother. I shrank back, feeling such an intruder. A figure loomed beside me, oh my stars, Madame Chatillon! Her lace and ribbons floated out around her like a cloud. Horrors, she'd start complaining and all the men would hear her and see me hiding there!

The French lady quite surprised me. She took in the scene at a glance and hastily shrank low, bringing a finger to her lips. Together, we tiptoed away, leaving the men to their conversation.

The first turn down the main road took us out of view of the men and right to the most picturesque view imaginable. The half-moon bay might have been a painting. The turn of the tide brought tiny, foaming waves around a beached dory and retreating, sweeping the beach clean.

Scraps of light shone through to glitter on the fog.

Madame placed her hand gently on my arm. "You are *tres* sensitive Mademoiselle Elizabeth, to show such discretion."

Amusingly, I happened to be thinking exactly the same thing about her.

"The men speak sadly of those far from home, no?" She gazed to the east. "It is sad. A sad time."

I hadn't thought of Madame's feeling at all. Suddenly, I felt quite heartless. "I'm sorry Madame. Of course, you are far from home, too."

She waved her elegantly long hands at the charming little bay in front of us. "When I see how the light glitters on each wave, I, too, think of home. I think of Monsieur Monet and how he captured light. I can hardly describe to those who have not the experience, of the play of light and shade he created, making the most ordinary scene aerial, spiritual." She waved her hands as if capturing the bay in a frame. "All my family loved *d'art.* It was our world. So much gone now, stolen from galleries and museums."

"You must miss home."

"Home, the family, the culture. From when I was very young, we attended *Le Académie* exhibitions." She brought her hand to her throat like an actress. "I loved it so." Madame Chatillon swept up her long, old-fashioned draped skirts off to one side and there, against the light and dark backdrop of the still-foggy sea, I could imagine her, as she must have appeared once: a pretty young debutant in a world of elegance and beauty, dressed to the height of fashion.

She must be very nearly the same age as Mrs. Trumbull, too. Funny how I could see them both as they must have been.

"I stood at the unveiling of Impression, *soleil levant et la Salon de Paris.*" She lifted both hands as if to embrace a huge painting on a wall. "Monsieur Monet was *magnifique*, a romantic figure for my family and all our circle. My father cleverly acquired several small, early landscapes by Monet. Our treasures." She stood there, frozen, staring out to sea, and suddenly her words became a torrent. "No, no my family is my treasure. Where are they? I watch every day, Elizabeth, the newspapers, and for letters. Ships have arrived, but not my grandson, not our treasures. They were preparing to book passage. There are few passenger ships so it must be one due in just days. These last few weeks I have heard no word at all!"

Her words tugged at my heart. Her grandson!

"Madame Chatillon," I stuttered, "I am so sorry."

"No, no, I do not ask for sorry, but what to do. Who do I ask? How do I find them?" She clutched her hands together and struggled to keep back tears. "The devils have not sunk their ship!"

"You've written, I take it?"

"Yes, to Marie, and also my eldest sister who remained in Giverny, though I begged her to come to safety."

"Still no word?"

"All summer I received letters, Marie kept careful check on opportunities to book passage on ships leaving port. Then all at once, nothing. The post mistress says all letters are delivered."

"Perhaps your family is on the way?"

"My sister would still be there. She did not plan to travel." Madame stared out to sea exactly as I had seen her stand and stare out our front room windows, these last weeks. "My son's wife will bring everything. All our treasures. We were careful to guard ours, where so many invested in works still in galleries when the invasion came. I have no money left Elizabeth. At the end of the summer, I had to tell Emmaline Brookeson that I awaited a shipment from home, and would settle my bill once it arrived. The Brookesons have been very good to wait."

Pale and elegant and desperate, she stood there, asking my advice and all I could suggest was…was… "Wait now. Didn't I see a letter for you in the tray two days ago?"

She nodded. "My son. He is in the service. He

thinks the family left to board a ship in Calais, but word should have come ahead. I should have seen names in passenger lists."

"We've not received every newspaper," I tried to sound reassuring, but suddenly, I remembered burnt newspapers in the smoking room fireplace and one of Madame's letters in the gentlemen's room mail tray.

I had an uncomfortable thought. "You let the Brookeson's know you were expecting money?"

"Yes, yes. I told Emmaline Brookeson. There are perhaps three of the grand old steamships going back and forth, bringing families and all their worldly goods to safety. They are not like the small ships, rushing willy-nilly, but proper big ships, with passenger lists, with holds large enough for goods and furnishings. They are secretive about their schedules for safety, but my sister watches and shares this with me."

A tiny fishing vessel eased into the bay before us. A trick of the light sent its shadow out onto the scraps of fog, beyond the harbor. The shadow loomed as if a huge ship bore down on our tiny harbor. I drew back and nearly gasped.

A cloud shifted, the Sun bore through full strength, and the shadow disappeared. It was quite an ordinary seaside scene again.

Madame took no notice. "I begged my son's wife, Marie, to book passage long ago. She tarried all summer, preparing, packing. Then suddenly, no word. No word from Giverny. My sister had told me every time she heard of a ship leaving port. Now, no word, these many weeks. I have not heard if the Folkestone has again departed from Calais." Her breath caught, almost on a sob, but she drew herself up and pressed her lips firmly together. "The waiting has been difficult."

I stood side-by-side with the French lady, as rays from the sun cast away the scraps of fog in the crystal clear, picture-perfect day and wondered at the play of light upon the water. Something seemed far from right; far, far from right.

Chapter Nine
Promising Fog

In the following days, things might have sunk back to ordinary, but somehow they missed the mark. Day after day, I found myself up early, watching the weather and reminding myself how Daro had promised to keep an eye on Oceanside.

One foggy gray not-quite-dawn, I spotted his familiar shape tying up at our dock. He stood stock still, staring east. I stole out the kitchen door and hustled along in near-darkness though I had no reason to rush out there or to speak to him. No good reason.

"Daro," I called from the flagstone walk.

He half-turned to me and smiled. "I was waiting for the Sun and here I find you instead."

I couldn't help but grin. "Will the Sun be on time this morning, sir?"

"*And I with the earth am moving into the light…*" he quoted softly, as if he commanded the great cloud of fog to sink soggily away from us.

"I'm afraid we won't see the sunrise this morning." I felt like dancing. The weather didn't matter at all. My sunshine stood right in front of me.

"*Even in the darkness below the Earth, the Earth brings our face to light.*" He motioned to the east. "Can't you feel it? My heart lifts as I feel our sky lighten, whether or not the light shines through."

Why no easy words would come to me as I stood by him, I could never tell. I felt the world lightening and my heart lifting more and more. I might have simply agreed, noted how the fog began to shimmer now and grow pale, but I could not find words to describe how it felt. I might as well be walking in a dream, for I floated lighter than the fog. I took his arm in silence and we stood, looking east.

He put his free hand over mine. "Your heart lifts, as well?"

I nodded, more and more lost in this foggy dream-world.

He turned us slightly southward. "In fog like this, I wait for the opening in the clouds to see the first of the rays. At such times, the light creates affects all unexpected. There are strange lights the fishermen all know about because they are up before the dawn to see such things: Glories, and sky halos, Sun dogs, and the like. It's the magic of light."

I thought of Madame's recollection of artworks as she looked out over the colorful sea. Two such different people inspired by the same sort of vision made me wonder at, as he said, 'the magic of light.'

South of us, the fog took on a scrappy look as it thinned over harbor. "Wait, now," Daro murmured

I might have stood beside him forever, as if we could be a couple and be utterly free of entanglements. I might be free from family expectation and follow him into the life of a wanderer. Wanderer. An emptiness loomed.

I stood in a fearful place suddenly, feeling not freedom but emptiness. I claimed I didn't want the well-planned life of a married woman, with family, duties, and everyday much like the next, yet to up-anchor, to throw cares into the wind and have no plan at all took me from quiet bay to dangerous seas indeed.

I must have clung to him as I contemplated those dangerous waters of our future.

He wrapped one arm around me. "Fear no storms today. The Sun is nearly here. I guessed it would clear, as soon as I saw you. There's a bluish halo today. It followed you down the path."

'He always knows the weather,' Cook had said, and 'Spent his young life in darkness.'

I imagined the mine, all darkness and shadows, and the only light was what each of the men carried for themselves.

"Those who've spent a long time in darkness know about light." I had no idea where my words came from. I might have quoted some long-ago line, I'd read, but they were true words for him and I could tell he thought so.

His eyes lifted as if he could see beyond the clouds. "Winters," he said at last, "Those short days. I'd be walking to work, and I'd suddenly feel the sun's approach. I'd hang back, hang back one more second, two, just to see the first rays come over the horizon. Later, when we finished our work day, it would already be dark when we came to the surface."

"Now you can sense the Sun even if she's hidden by clouds." My words lacked his pure poetic phrasing.

He placed his hand at my waist as naturally as if we had stepped together to dance. I placed my palm in his. The rhythm of waves and the cries of gulls wove together and we swept around in a buoyant little circle, in a waltz all our own.

"Is this real, this hour upon a beach, under the wide-open sky? Where do we go from here?"

"*Where thou goest I shall go*," I quoted softly. It was rash, but seemed fitting. Only after I spoke and I saw his stunned look, did I think on the full meaning of the words.

My dance partner looked gravely down at me. It was his turn to be tongue-tied, apparently. We gazed into one another's eyes. The morning might have been lost, or the day. Truly, all sense of time drifted away.

The day's light glittered through to light upon us in this fog-shrouded world. I forgot about being too bold, forgot to worry. I too could find inspiration in the light.

"Captain," Daro said. "Walk with me."

I strolled arm in arm with him, along the beach. Objects loomed as strange, pale shadows, mysteries until we stood right by them.

Daro paced along as always, escorting me along a beach I knew as well as my own bedroom. "Elizabeth," he said as we skirted an overturned dory, "are you minding your step?"

"I do not believe I am, Mr. Michelson."

We eased up the sands together to skirt a particularly far-reaching wave.

"Should I be?" I thought to ask.

"I should think so. No, I can have no idea what to think." He patted my hand. "You arrived like light, and my heart lifted, and I've no idea what might come next."

His heart lifted! Oh, his heart lifted! Finally he spoke about how he felt! My own bubbled like the froth of a wave.

"A moment is but a moment." His voice deepened.

"I cannot change light, or bend the Sun to my will, but Captain you swept up like light itself and took my hand. Still, there is much in me, I do not wish to change or do not wish to lose."

I did not understand, but his tone was grave and he was certainly trying to tell me something. Warning and sorrow filled his words. I felt the magic of the dream world fall away from us.

Still, I struggled to hold onto the moment. "I would not see you change, Daro."

"I cannot say what the future will bring. I can make no promise."

A single edge of wave slipped above its fellows to touch swirl about our boots. I laughed. "Why, who can say, about any future? Us, along this beach, no more than those who march to war."

"True." He escorted me back to Oceanside, to my job and my life, without further poetry.

I tumbled forward into what had become an ordinary day enclosed in the walls at the once-magical Oceanside.

****

I dashed up the main hall stairway with a plan to straighten up the two small guestrooms at the rear. Beryl could simply not do all of the housekeeping, even for the few guests left. I pulled the extra quilt off the bed and stored in the 'spares' closet and set about dusting. Sometimes, mindless tasks allow the mind to wander, and in my case, so often given to fanciful notions.

I fear it was but few minutes before I imagined dashing about a different house altogether.

Mrs. Trumbull's house, somehow grander than

Oceanside, had intrigued me since my first glimpse inside. I had no trouble imagining it at all. I might stand in the narrow hallway of Oceanside, but in my mind, I dashed along her grand entranceway.

The main hall's decoration combined art and furniture; paintings on the walls offered brightness above the dark mahogany side tables, carved banisters and freshly aired throw rugs carefully placed. No cobwebs lurked in her high corners. It was all light and airy and lovely. A candle sat burning mid-window, as if on watch, even in the full light of day.

I clasped my hands before the candle. Mrs. Trumbull! What a beautiful, tragic story. Here she's spent her lifetime tending her house and her lights. The gleaming lights along the widow's walk had saved us the day we brought *Thistle* up the coast. All her life, she had kept the candles burning in memory of, or perhaps in the hopes of the return of, the greatest and only love of her life. Captain Trumbull.

I confessed early on my weakness for tragic romance, didn't I? I am afraid I'd had little time for reading and less for gossip all this long season. One could hardly blame me for a touch of imaging. It was so terribly romantic in a way, to think she'd tended her walkway lights for so terribly long. She must have so loved her husband.

Her home must be laid out like the best of the Victorians of her day. I could see the upstairs landing as if I were there. Plainly, the master bedroom would sit to the right. Green I decided; a mint-green room with a large mint-green quilt. I tiptoed hesitantly across the threshold. The plump pillows and thick coverlet almost spoke to me. I took one moment to press down into the soft, soft bed and could have tumbled straight down into it. Even the quilt, one of those obviously made from a collection of oddments, felt soft.

A pair of framed silhouettes looked at one another over the top of the vast double bed, the old fashioned sort with elegant posts, all carved into pineapple shapes.

Indeed it had to be them; the Trumbulls. I could see the missus' pert nose, and her hair dressed high and elegantly. He, with his squared off beard and high forehead was the very picture of the old-time sea captain.

They were mounted and framed side-by-side, looking ever at one another. In the window next to them, I could see the sea, the great crashing waves and imagine this man…setting off, and she, Mrs. Trumbull, a young married woman, watching him go. She had expected him to return of course. She had waited…and waited.

I clutched my hands before me. Had word ever come? Had she some notion of what sea claimed her love? Oh, if but one letter could have gotten through! I must have reached out to them, or particularly to him; suddenly, he turned and gazed at me.

The heavy quilts in my hands plunked to the floor and fear I must have followed them down, for but a moment later, I pulled my face up out of the bedclothes. Fainted! Quite ridiculous.

No sea captain stood commandingly there, nor, indeed, do Mrs. Trumbull's elegant mint-green room surround me. I had imagined my way all around one of the hotel's mid-priced rooms. Understated beige was brightened by one small seaside print. The two windows looked southeast, not due east, like the

Trumbull home.

Still, the sea is the sea. I took myself to the window, to the magnificence framed between simple cloth curtains, and thought this, the everlasting blue, the white-caps and the ever-changing view all vastly more impressive than any of my imaginings.

"She never fit in here, did she?" The captain stood there, hands clasped behind his back, glaring at me from an entirely imaginary wall painting.

I had gone short on sleep one night too many. Still. It felt only right to tell him.

"She's done all right," I said."I mean, all right for herself. Became a schoolmarm, earned the respect of all."

Captain Trumbull's face looked so like an old time sea captain, for he was high browed and bearded. Yet, he sent me a good-humored gaze and, impossibly, very young and dashing. Oh! Of course he was. He had departed still a young man, and had stayed like that, all the years Mrs. Trumbull aged. As he looked away south it came to me, what she had said about me not being one of them.

"You two were like Daro and me, weren't you?" I mused aloud. "She wasn't one of you, but it didn't matter, didn't matter at all, because she had you. Then when you didn't come home, well, it did."

He clasped his hands and shook his head.

"She was left all alone here when you didn't come home."

The blue silhouette did not look my way.

"She told me, you know? Told me I might never be part of things here. I suppose she wanted me to know the risk. If something happens to Daro, I'm all alone here."

I stepped closer to the window. "She could have gone home, couldn't she?" The perfect blue of the crystal sky filled the window, and there, out there, I could almost see a big whaling ship riding the tide in toward the bay. How often had Mrs. Trumbull stared to the east, hoping against hope to see his ship coming in? "She couldn't leave for the longest time, because she so hoped. She stood here, waiting and waiting, looking for your ship, and then, then as hope faded…she'd stayed so long, she couldn't imagine leaving." Sadness seemed to tip into me like water pouring in from a pitcher.

"And she was gorgeous and faithful, and such a romantic, tragic story for all the locals to share, but then, really, still, all alone."

The blue swirled all around, and I lifted my gaze, guessing it might be one of those weird atmospheric affects you get up here, but I was merely lifting my gaze from face-down in the green and blue quilt.

I looked around the room. No portraits hung on these walls, no one stood glaring at me.

I gathered up the quilt, hefted them onto a hip, and set off down the stairs.

Ariel stood at the hearth, looking cold. "They called luncheon a moment ago, did you hear?" She seemed no more real than the stern, dashing captain.

****

"Lemonade?" Mrs. Brookeson glanced around the luncheon table.

Knowing Madame Chatillon's secret as I did, especially knowing how she was allowed to remain without cost and with not one wit less service than before, I felt much more kindly toward our proprietor

Mrs. Brookeson. Lunch today had a warmer aura.

"Let me fetch the pitcher." I popped out to the kitchen. Beryl shadowed me, not so much helping, but skulking in my wake. She crunched on something as I reached for the tray of drinks.

"What have you got there, Beryl? If there are crackers to go out, too, I'll be happy to take them."

She shrugged, all hunched over as if I'd caught her out. Anyone would think she had been stealing, or she'd swallowed someone's diamond ring. After a second, she admitted, "Candy almond."

I clearly recalled the glass dish of Jordan almonds sailing off into a corner, during the other day's crazy scramble.

"They got thrown off, thrown away," she blurted.

"It's all right," I assured her.

"Cook had me clean up in there. Was all a mess. There weren't but a couple candies left." She swallowed. "Papers and map and stuff all wet. I didn't know what to do with it all."

"You knew what to do with the candy, though, I take it. I hope you didn't eat the ones on the floor," I stressed, but she probably did. Fancy candies like that hardly fell her way ordinarily.

She frowned and did not meet my eye. If Beryl didn't want to say something, you could hardly get a word out of her.

"If there are any more, you wipe them off real careful before you eat them. Don't say one word about anything going on in that room to anyone else, hear?"

Beryl grinned. "There's always pieces of cigars or bits of cigarettes in there, but never candy. And never any pretty stuff before, just old copies of The Cape

Courier or that one cent paper from Halifax."

"Was there a drink?" The missus whined from the dining room.

"Just getting lemonade," I called. I grabbed Beryl's arm. "What do you mean, 'pretty stuff?'"

From the wide front pocket of her apron, she drew a sparkly silver ribbon like you'd use to fasten a gift box. Beryl plopped it into my hand and stood with her head hanging. "I thought I'd keep it for a hair ribbon," she whispered.

The ribbon was very pretty, and probably expensive, but little more than a scrap. I handed it back to Beryl. "I don't think anyone will miss it, and it will look very nice as a hair ribbon."

Osten interrupted. "Were you bringing a drink? People are having their sandwiches."

"Yes, yes." I hefted the pitcher. "I'll pour right now."

Beryl slid passed.

"And not a word from you," I cautioned her.

Osten paused in the doorway, wanting to ask.

"No need for any discussion of poor Genevieve, I should think," I said briskly, as if I'd been worried about gossip.

"Oh, quite right Miss Eames. Quite right."

Chapter Ten
Seeking Information

Our big bay mare strolled beside me to the end of her paddock then spun and bucked when she reached the limits of her fence line.

"Adieu Anslee-mare," I called to her. I walked straight back through the wide field of scrawny, browning marsh grass and climbed the first of the hills on the way to Alma's.

Left behind, the mare still snorted and pranced. She'd have liked nothing better than a run through the wide-open fields with me. It was enough of a walk for me to wish I'd ridden, before I reached even halfway. I paused at the footbridge over the stream to catch my breath. I felt quite undone by the view.

The vivid, green-hued hills, now hoary gray with early frost, rose as giants far inland, impressive but intimidating. They were less welcoming than the charming seaside and mostly untroubled by tourists, or any others, so far as I knew. They had been mere shadows on the stormy morn when we had run to Alma's for safety.

Evergreen branches glittered with tiny icicles, marking the edge of an old, old forest. Some part of me felt the wildness in there, a wildness not unlike that which harbored in the sea. A great, great presence sat in the shadows of those trees, an awareness, perhaps the soul of the island itself.

Oh, how entirely fanciful! Still, the place inspired it. A poet might gaze inland here and find verses springing to mind, or a musician discover a symphony. You might think the aesthetic sensibilities of our resident artist might occasionally turn to this sublime landscape of steep hills and distant peaks, as well.

I suddenly wanted to explore those hazy jumbled peaks. Today, however, luncheon hovered over the back of my mind and spurred me onward. I needed to be back in time to help or else Cook would have to do it all. Beryl had been assigned to clean upstairs and would not be spared to help.

Alma's swept doorway welcomed, although by the time I reached it, I was plodding. Had I truly run this whole way during the storm? It seemed utterly impossible.

Alma popped out as I approached. "Elizabeth, oh how grand of you to call. My Donall took a two-week job up north and I've been without an adult to talk to these last few days. My word, he nearly accepted the position for the whole winter, but I wouldn't have it. Two weeks is long enough. I am already longing for his return and little Donnie's asking for him every single day. Can you visit long?"

I stopped at the wooden arch over the lintel. "I've actually come with a purpose."

"Do come in and I'll put the tea on." Alma towed me into the warmth of her kitchen.

"I'm afraid I can't stay." I plumped down on that quilt-covered chair by the fire and felt as if I were melting into the soft cushiony warmth. It was an effort to keep my eyes open. This would never do. I leaned forward. "I'm afraid I've come to ask you something."

"Yes, yes of course."

"It's gossip, nasty gossip really, but I assure you I do have good reason for asking."

Alma paused with one hand grasping the tea kettle over the stove. "Oh?"

"One of our maids, Siobhan, went home quite abruptly this summer. She was not an inadequate maid, or had any complaint made about her."

Alma began poking the fire up rather briskly. Too briskly.

"I've never heard Beryl say one bad word about her," I said.

"I should think not." Alma fiddled with a potholder and turned away.

"But I bet she mentioned it to you. Did she know why Siobhan left?"

"I canna think it right to speak of the gal's misfortune."

"It's not the maid I am concerned about, although I think what I heard is a shame, if true. It's the devil that got her into trouble that I'm interested in. I want to know if Avery Brookeson is to blame."

"Hardly makes a difference now." Alma kept fussing around the stove.

"It might make a difference to Avery. In fact, it should make a difference to Avery." I chose my words carefully. "You see, one of the guests has threatened to share this piece of gossip in order to disgrace Avery. His behavior certainly wouldn't be accepted, in the rather upright social circles of Halifax, nor yet with his church, but only if it were true, of course."

"You're looking for evidence to ruin the man?"

"Actually, no. I just want to know if it's true. He departed, very quickly, merely at the threat."

Alma nodded, still not looking at me.

I felt the need to explain. "Even if the gossip about Siobhan and Avery were true, it seems uncharacteristic for Avery to give up so easily. His sudden departure seems suspicious." I didn't think I was making headway. "If the gossip I heard is not true, then I am very worried, because he is up to some sort of a trick."

Alma deliberately strolled over and sat beside me. She leaned over the stack of newspapers piled between us, glanced down, hesitated and finally said, "It is private, and nasty gossip besides, but I suppose, when you look at all the horror going on in this world, it is petty matter." She clasped her hands together. "Beryl did tell me when Siobhan got sent home. It wasn't anything to do with her getting into shameful trouble herself. Siobhan accidentally walked in on this Avery and a guest, a Mrs. Fromart. In the bedroom. You know how I mean. Siobhan got paid not to mention it and packed off straightaway."

"So there was something." I leaned back in the chair. "Something yet nothing. It's not something we could prove, not like an out-of-wedlock child. He had no real reason to depart."

"No one would want that gossip to spread."

I shrugged. "It would only be a rumor. An affair, with only a maid as witness? That would not make Avery depart suddenly. It must have suited him to leave." I thought of the times he'd gone off, to 'stay in Ingonish.' His disappearances looked more and more suspicious. Avery could have laughed at our threats and kept right on courting Gen.

"Perhaps he decided to be kind and do as you wished?" Alma went to see to the kettle.

"Kind does not describe Avery. No, he had no reason to go, no reason to let us think we had won, yet he'd gone meekly. He must have wanted to leave without arousing comment."

Alma set my tea at my elbow. "Look at those papers. All that horror over in Europe. There are whole families desperate to get out. You can hardly square the lives of the folks at your fancy resort with the awful goings-on in this world."

It was true. There were many newspaper accounts of desperate families squashing into tiny quarters aboard old vessels, in an effort to escape.

She patted the top article. "I've been reading about folks who haven't enough money to book passage out for their families, so send their youngsters off alone, to what they hope will be safety. I've heard of Mums sewing a few dollars into a child's collar and packing crackers for the long uncomfortable days aboard ship. I can't imagine sending my little Donnie off, then waiting and waiting for word, looking for a letter, praying the ship would make it to safe harbor somewhere, hoping some kind soul would take him in."

Safe harbor. Like the Madame's family, aiming here for safe harbor. Many families were trying to come here to safety. As Alma touched a tissue to her eyes, a dreadful feeling swept over me.

What had Daro said about false lights set to lure ships in for their plunder? A shipload of treasures…and children?

****

I left a tad late on the sparkling crisp day, feeling

far too full of tea and scones and not eager to get back to Oceanside. I wished I could take the afternoon and gallop Ainslee mare on up to McLellan's Harbor and contrive a few minutes visit with a certain gentleman. I was needed in the kitchen to help Cook. Heaven knew she didn't want to be doing extra.

I forgot all about her and my assorted duties as I topped the little knoll and looked down at the footbridge.

Daro stood looking inland at the deep dark forest. Though light sparkled crystal-clear all around him, his shadow obscured all else beyond.

He might well be a visitor from some ancient legend, standing there, surveying a land of lesser mortals. I could see him as a ship's captain from days of old, fierce and brave, with a great booming laugh.

I am being fanciful again, I thought. He looked my way and smiled, and all at once, shrank down to more human proportions. I stepped along to meet him on the bridge where I had first sensed the odd enchantment of Cape Breton Island. Salty sea scented air met the hint of pine from the mighty trees inland, and the little creek marked the bridge between the two.

Daro folded his arms across his chest and nodded as I approached. He spoke the one word, "Captain."

I guessed he was here for something serious.

"I need you to remind me of what you saw, exactly what you saw, when we turned the sailboat that first time, south of the point."

I'd hoped for some more, but what? A friendly, even familiar gesture? "The point," I repeated, quite stupidly.

"I've been thinking on this false light. I know I've

cast my mind back to Mother Stewart's readings of the awful tales of wreckings. There's a thrill to those verses, all talk of hauntings and revenge. I remember those best from when I was a boy, and maybe I am too quick to call them to mind. One minute I think it possible, the next, ridiculous. Tricking mariners into shallow waters. Who here, living on the edge of the sea, would ever do such a thing?"

"Unthinkable," I murmured. "There's been no other such light, since? No other boats have reported anything?"

"I did ask others here, fisherman. They've not seen it, nor think my concern likely."

"Did you tell them about Mrs. Trumbull's missing oil?"

"They don't want to hear warnings from me. I might-a come from McLellan's but I grew up down in Sydney Mines." Daro glared at his feet. "What they think of me is neither here nor there. The thing is, I can't be sure wrecking is what's intended. I could be mistaken."

"I saw the false light from *Thistle,* too." I assured him. "It fooled me."

"Does it mean wrecking, though?" he mused. "For that matter, what can I do about it? I mean, I can't guard the coast."

"Who does guard our coast?"

"None who would thank me for fanciful reports." He looked up suddenly. "There are good guards; the official coast patrol, naval military vessels, fisherman, lighthouse keepers and watchers of all sorts up and down the coast. Maybe there is not so much for me to worry about."

"I am afraid I haven't given it any thought at all." I touched his hand. "I'm still caught up with the very minor doings at Oceanside, and of one unimportant but unfortunate romance."

He made a face.

"It is a worthy cause. Poor Genevieve is a lovely person, who needs help getting away from…"

Daro chuckled. "I think you might want to reconsider meddling with other people's romances. In the old poems, that sort of thing never turns out well."

We started back toward the resort—hopefully, for my part. I so longed for him to speak of his feelings. As he had sought me out this time, surely he meant to speak in some romantic manner? I wanted to stand and talk with Daro on the picturesque bridge forever and ever. The place itself inspired courtship. He would perhaps start with a quote from a poet, in his deep rolling voice. I almost held my breath, waiting for words with some hint of affection.

"What about where watchers are few?" he suddenly asked. "The coastal guards watch the populated places and stand ready to defend good harbors."

"Stands to reason." I sighed. "Not much sense in protecting the empty highlands or rocky shoals."

"Rocky shoals are exactly what a wrecker would need. Truth is, whole stretches of coast are unwatched because they are dangerous areas. We worry about keeping enemy ships from invading, not about them galloping into rocks." He nodded slowly. "The immigrant ships mostly make their way to New Brunswick around our northern tip. Up there, people are sparse. To lure a ship onto shoals, why I'd go even farther up than Meat Cove, to a place like Trouble Cove. It didn't get its name for no reason. Its rocks would ground a deep-water vessel and make for easy plunder."

"Still, even if you've guessed right, you cannot guess when a ship will be going by, or if it will be a ship with a valuable cargo. Not without knowing all the ship's schedules." The words, 'ship schedules' brought another conversation to my mind. Madame Chatillon had said she received information on passenger ships in her letters. Those selfsame letters that had recently gone missing.

"Poor weather conditions would be the most obvious time," Daro was saying. "Fog or storm. Still, the wrecker would have to be lucky or have some early notice of the approach of a passenger vessel."

"Mmmm? Early notice of a passenger ship?" Again, Daro's comment called to mind Madame Chatillon's words. She had said her sister ordinarily sent word about the ships her grandson might be expected to travel onboard. Would those letters have enough information for a wrecker? In my mind's eye, I could see the French Lady's mail sitting on Avery's desk. Could that account for her 'missing' letters?

I could scarcely credit my sudden, horrible thought.

"Wreckers would want to be sure to lure in a passenger ship, with goods, not say, a fishing boat, or coast patrol," Daro mused, but my mind galloped ahead, trying to sort possibilities.

We walked together back to Oceanside. Daro did not offer me his hand. Perhaps his thoughts were entirely taken up with worry. Perhaps he gave no thought to me at all. I could hardly make sense of my own thoughts.

We walked in silence.

I had so wished for another visit with Daro and now this lucky meeting had caught me unprepared. I struggled to think of conversation. It was my own fault if the poor man never gave me one word or hint of encouragement! Yet, any such light conversation would seemed frivolous in the face of the monstrous crime we both contemplated, wouldn't it?

We topped the small hill behind the resort, and he stopped quite naturally to view the magnificence of sea and sky before us. Perfect blue and while waves rolled, one after the other, up the sands of the crescent beach. The light sparkled along the underside of the clouds like a spattering of crystals. Softly, Daro quoted "the flying cloud, the frosty light."

He did not so much as glance my way, but his hand suddenly grasped mine.

****

My heart still fluttered like a butterfly as I slipped in the main door. There had been no elaborate goodbyes, no words or promises and yet, we'd shared moments, long moments.

Ariel nearly leapt out of the foyer with a paper in her hand. "Where have you been? Look, Gen left me this."

I squashed the urge to turn and run.

"I don't believe this for one second." Ariel shook the note under my nose.

Surely, I could have one day without these petty guest problems? I dutifully took the note and read, in Gen's elegant hand,

Ariel, I am going to stay in Ingonish. I'm waiting

for a few things from the dressmakers, and I want a few days on my own. I'll be ready to go home in a few days, don't be mad, Gen.

"Surely this is good Ariel, I mean, if she's getting ready to go back to Halifax?"

"This is not like her. She's up to something." Ariel took back the note. "I expected her to be sitting around whining for days."

Beryl scooted past with a full trash bin, humming the old Barbara Allen song. Dust trailed in her wake. She'd have been dismissed ages ago, if she weren't the last maid left. She was completely unmindful of how it looked to have a scruffy maid hauling debris out the front door.

"Barbara Allen." Ariel pressed her hands over her mouth. "A sign."

Nonsense," I said. "Doesn't mean a thing. Probably Beryl's favorite song, it being so romantic."

"With the lovers dying for one another," Ariel almost sobbed.

Oh, dear, why did she have to leap to the dark ending? Still, there was no point in endlessly reassuring her. I gave up and set off for the kitchen. The sound of metallic clicking of the wireless made me stop abruptly. I hesitated outside the doorway to the smoking room.

Ariel shook her head. "It's not Avery in there. Mark DelaMore. He's been hanging over the wireless all day."

"Really?" I tiptoed to the door. Inside, the wireless chattered, but without any background conversation. I eased open the door.

Mark hunched on the footstool by the wireless contraption. He glanced over his shoulder at the sound of the door, then rose quickly in a gentlemanly fashion.

I held out a hand. "Don't get up. I didn't see you at lunch, and thought perhaps you'd like sandwiches brought in?" I scanned every dark corner, but the room sat empty, apart from Mark.

"Very thoughtful of you, Elizabeth. I haven't wanted to leave these latest reports."

"News from overseas?" I guessed.

"A massing of armaments, battle expected. Oh, nothing for you lasses to worry about, of course. I'd be pleased if you could send in a tray so I can keep listening."

'Nothing for you lasses to worry about' indeed. As if women couldn't perfectly well follow news reports. I stomped over to the front and grabbed a dish to put something together for him.

Cook marched by with a large tray of deviled crab and crackers. They joined a salad and a few slices of bread on the side buffet there in the foyer.

"I'm sorry I was held up, Mrs. Buxton."

Our patient cook silently motioned toward the front hall to where Madame Chatillon stood by the narrow window staring out to sea. She had received no letter again, apparently.

I wondered why Cook made such a point about our French lady standing there. The fancy crab salad would certainly suit the Madame, although she'd hardly make a fuss about it. No, Cook meant to tell me something.

Ariel trotted after me and clutched at my arm. "What should we do?"

I couldn't think of a thing to do about Gen, and I had the uncomfortable feeling I had missed something. One too many things were going on. I squirmed away from Ariel and hurried back to the kitchen. Cook stood over the oven, carefully lifting the edges of scones to check their bottoms.

"Is everything all right, Mrs. Buxton?"

"Discreet of you. Keeping all the French Woman's story to yourself." Cook began easing the scones off the hot pan with a spatula. "She's waiting for her grandson. You knew all along? Her boy in the midst of the war and young grandson anywhere."

"Yes."

"I thought she considered herself too grand for us, but here, she's been waiting and waiting. She's kept her dignity. Can't say that about all." I knew Cook meant to compare the French woman to Mrs. Brookeson, who could pitch a screaming fit like a three year old.

I held my fingers out over the warming oven. Much more had been going on at this hotel than I had suspected. And somehow, I was still here. Avery must have told his mother something about what had happened, but Mrs. Brookeson had not said a word to me about the incident. She was apparently determined that all should appear to be carrying on as if normal.

Cook eased a large loaf of bread out of the oven. "I'll not be surprised if we don't have another storm coming. Daro always seems to know. This morning, he said the color of sunrise gave him an uneasy feeling."

"I think we're better prepared this time," I assured her. I so wanted a few moments peace, to think. I wanted to remember my own visit with Daro.

"I'm baking a meat pie for tomorrow. It will only need heating. Might be, I stay home." Cook hustled around, busy as always.

"You left your lucky stone behind, last time," I

pointed out. "Maybe you better take it with you tonight."

'Harrumph." She straightened and shot me a look as though she were irritated, but said, "Next time, you take the bluestone. Can't hurt to keep luck with you."

"Shouldn't you have it?"

She pushed me toward the door. "You go along and think about something else entirely."

Chapter Eleven
Decisions

Dawn brought overcast skies and a strange, deepening dark to the day. I set to work in the kitchen, making coffee and setting out toast.

I looked at the bluestone there at the hearth. Silly, I know, but I felt good about it. Cook thought more of me than she had ever let on, and she was a tough one, so I was more than a little proud.

Cook was more disdainful of Mrs. Brookeson than she had ever let on before, too. Still, Mrs. Brookeson was nobody's fool. With that in mind, I uneasily had to admit that Oceanside's owners had some other purpose for keeping the resort open.

Madame Chatillon had told Mrs. Brookeson that she regularly received letters with news of wealthy refugees aboard ships; ships that might well be described as treasure ships. The ships carried artworks and valuable household furnishings rescued from the old country, all part of individual families' treasures. Likely, every ship carried a fortune and they traveled by our very shores.

The Brookeson's shouldn't need a fortune, but many of the wealthy s in this part of the world had invested overseas. Much of value had been lost to the German invasion. Lately, Oceanside hadn't managed to pay all its bills. The fact seemed ominous.

Mrs. Brookeson had decided to stay on here, near a place where ships passed relatively secluded shores, on their way to the ports of New Brunswick on the Canadian mainland. She had also, rather suddenly in the middle of the summer, encouraged a romance between her son and the wealthy Genevieve, who she previously detested.

Mid-summer, the battle of the Somme had spread from Verdun and ravaged France. I had little grasp of distant geography, but whole cities and villages had fallen. Likely, fortunes had been lost right then, both in property and in art, as well as other investments. In times of war, all those with their chief investments overseas stood to lose their fortunes.

What if, sometime this summer, the Brookesons had lost their fortune? Suddenly, the idiotic heiress might seem like a good choice as a bride. And, when they heard of the fortunes sailing right past their shores in the shape of various treasure ships, I guess they might have decided to claim someone else's fortune for themselves.

I shuddered at the thought. Although I could not be sure, their behavior and all the events of late certainly suggested I was correct.

Beryl shuffled into the kitchen. "Daro says we should go to Alma's today. Barometer's falling. I know my Auntie Alma is happy to have you come and stay, too."

Beryl stood there shivering on stone floor, no doubt remembering her auntie's pumpkin muffins and the rich warmth of her kitchen. She would not be unhappy to scoot up there.

"Is Daro here?"

"He stopped early this morning. Sent Old George south on some errand. He just went down to the beach to pull in the resort's dory." She scowled.

"Is there more?"

"He's got to go north he said. He needs to take some provisions. I'm to pack him a bread and a big square of cheese. I'm not sure where he's going." Beryl put her hands in her apron pocket and kept her gaze down. "It can't be good weather for travel."

I barely nodded. Daro hadn't even waited for a word with me. I sighed and stumbled forward woodenly. I had to face the truth. I had been fooling myself from the start. My heart sank and I could hardly feel my fingers and I wanted nothing more than to go hide in my room for a good cry.

I fumbled my sweater off the chair back by the stove. "Put this on and muffle up proper, overcoat and scarf, Beryl. Going over the fields to Alma's is going to feel like a long walk, today."

"Ain't you coming?"

"No." I hesitated, but it couldn't hurt for her to know. "I'll go north too, whether he wants me or not. You can pack some extra food for me, if you would."

I couldn't allow myself to give in to such ridiculous emotion. Whether or not Daro felt anything for me, I knew I had to do my part to stop what was coming. I believed I'd figured this out, this wrecking. It had to be Avery. Darned if I would sit back while someone else struggled to stop him.

"Barometer's falling." Daro stomped in from the yard. "Overcast. Flat calm sea. Something is brewing. I need to be off north. I think the weather coming in might be right for wrecking."

I didn't glance up. "You aren't going alone."

"This isn't like a day sailing, miss."

"It's Elizabeth, not 'miss.' I'll go along or go alone if you don't take me with you."

He shifted his feet. "I'm going fast and overland. You can't help. It might be just some local fellow, desperate. A man I can reason with."

"No. It's Avery. It must be. If it is him, he won't be going alone, I can tell you."

Daro frowned. "Avery? The fellow due to inherit all this? I can't see it."

"I can. I don't know why it took me so long to realize. It's likely all the Brookesons. Its Avery and his mother both. It would explain everything. I think they have run out of money, either had poor business ventures or have lost their investments overseas."

"They own this huge place," he said, disbelieving.

Beryl stood stock-still in the middle of the kitchen and gaped at me. She would carry this news up to Alma's, wouldn't she? I could not stop myself from blurting out my suspicions even so; heaven help me if I had guessed wrong.

"Who knows if this place is paid for? And, it looks like any one of those passenger ships might well be carrying a fortune in artworks," I argued.

Daro did not look convinced. Beryl simply looked shocked.

"In both of the last storms, Avery went off somewhere. He has a detailed map of the coast, listens to the wireless for news of incoming bad weather, and I think he's been checking Madame Chatillon's letters for the dates ships set sail from France. I suspect he's the one who stole Mrs. Trumbull's lamp mirror and oil.

It all adds up. He's planning wrecking. There is no other explanation."

Daro stared at me as if wondering if I had gone completely mad. It took him nearly a minute to admit, "A possibility."

"Probability," I retorted. "Shall we try to gather some helpers?"

"I sent a note to the coastal patrol chief at Ingonish about the false light." The big man frowned. "I hope he will warn all vessels in the area."

"Why wouldn't he send out word?"

"Because it was only me telling him. Sounds a little far-fetched, doesn't it? Purposefully causing shipwreck?" He eased toward the door. "George carried the message south to him, though."

"Do you think the wreck will be at McLellan's harbor?"

Daro raised his eyebrows. "Why would you think of McClellans?"

"I think Avery practiced his fake 'lighthouse' idea on us, the day we took the *Thistle* up to the harbor."

"Practice." A dark look crossed his features. "He might have killed us both. You think of that? Do you really think he's that dangerous?"

"I think he could be ruthless. He cares for no one but himself. Do you suppose he'll try to lure a ship in below McClellan's?"

"No, no one would want to crash a big ship in there. There are too many folk about to see, either to catch him red-handed or to help rescue people. No, he needs seclusion and time to salvage all the goods. No, whoever it is, I see Trouble Cove as the most likely spot. There are other possible locations, but I can't check them all."

"Can George take us north?"

"The coastal road would take too long and, at this point, we might not get through. No. Pack me some bread and I'll travel straight up and over the island."

Our Beryl might have been dumbstruck about our suspicions, but feeding folks she could handle. She heaved Cook's enormous meat pie onto the counter. "How about this? None of the ladies will want beef pie, and none of the men are left here."

"None of the men are here? Mr. Osten? Mark, that is to say, Mr. DeLaMore?" I swept over to the counter.

"They left straightaway after breakfast, yesterday. Mr. Osten had Old George start the Packard for him. It ain't back." She made a face. "I was watching for him, 'cause I was going to ask him for a ride."

"The professor?"

"He's upstairs, but he won't care for this. I'll make him a sandwich." Beryl set to swaddling the pie in kitchen cloths.

I shooed her aside. "I'll see to it. You go along right now."

Daro put his hand on my shoulder. "You take Beryl and get to Alma's. Both of you keep out of this place until I get back. Just in case."

"Did you hear what she said? None of the men left. All Avery's cohorts have gone to assist him!" I suppose I sounded that determined. Beryl knew I wasn't about to take no for an answer.

She pulled her bulky-sleeved woolen coat from the closet and deliberately handed it to me. "This'ud be better for traveling than yours. Mittens in the pocket."

"Oh Beryl, how sweet."

Daro shook his head firmly. "No."

Calmly, as if I had done this dozens of times, I said, "Get the horse ready and I'll finish packing the food."

****

I prepared in a matter of minutes and darted down the snowy avenue to meet Daro at the bridge. A light shower of snowflakes swirled around Oceanside, the meadow, and the low trees struggling against the wind.

Ainslee-mare's hooves clattered on the bridge.

"Running off with some poorly thought-of local man." Daro pulled up the horse right in the middle of the bridge and glared down at me. "Had you thought of what people will say?"

"I'm going." I started across the bridge. "Avery won't be alone, he'll have helpers. The men from the resort most likely. And maybe more too, had you thought of that? None of the fine fellows will be slogging into the sea to claim the cargo. Can you imagine any of them doing all that work? No, he'll have some hired men to do all the salvage."

"We don't really know it's him."

"Whoever, then. You might still need help. Or someone to send for help."

He allowed the mare to take a few more steps in my wake. "This is nothing you can help with. Better you should get a message to have some men follow me. If you bring word up to McClellan's, at least there'd be a hope that either you or George might convince a few to join me."

"Then there's Genevieve. She's gone with him, I bet." I walked right along. "Can you deal with her?"

Nothing but slow hoof beats answered my query

about Gen.

I didn't glance back. I didn't know which way to go once on the other side. I walked off the bridge feeling as if I were stepping off into nothingness. If he didn't come along, I had no idea which direction to turn.

The mare clopped off the bridge after me. Daro said, as if it were the most ordinary thing in the world, "It's going to be a hard climb, right up and over all those hills."

"We managed together on the *Thistle*." I didn't know if I should stay on the path or aim dead ahead for that one pointy peak.

"My way lies to north and west, in an ascent from the glen at the foot of the Sleeper's Waterfall. It is the fastest way, but it will be cold and difficult."

"You're sure this is where we should go?"

"It's the high point above the northernmost point of the island. If the man intent on shipwreck isn't at Trouble Cove, from there, we might be able to spot where he is."

"Do you think Avery came this way? All this climbing?"

"I'd guess he took the coast road with that big automobile and a lot of gear. Easier, but it's the long way 'round. He had a long head start."

Avery had had a long head start, because Ariel's threat had sent him away. I bet he had been planning to go the whole time.

I took a step, as if I knew which way. "You're sure of the way?"

"I know the way to the waterfall." He leaned down and offered me his hand. "Not arguing for hours might help us make better time."

I reached up and took his hand. We paused there a moment—truly, for less than the time for a breath. Yet, a shiver ran up my spine and he gazed down at me as if he too, felt it.

My face felt warm suddenly and I had to look away. I fumbled at his foot, looking for a stirrup, but without any comment, he swung me easily up behind him. As I shifted for a comfortable spot on the blanket, I saw the mare had no saddle—just this one thick blanket over her back.

"It will be hard to stay on," I pointed out.

"Hold on, Elizabeth." He did not glance back at me, but repeated, "Elizabeth."

The mare stepped off into a lovely big trot and, like the best of her ilk, her comfortable, softly jouncing gait swept us forward at a great pace.

Chapter Twelve
The Journey

The mare's prancing raised my spirits. I had discovered riding, like sailing, back at Mrs. Pritchard's school. Young ladies 'in the old country,' were well acquainted with racing and hunting. We were meant to develop some basic level of competence in such 'upper crust' activities.

I'd loved riding, like sailing, far too well for my interest to be considered ladylike.

Sitting behind Daro on the broad-backed mare posed no challenge. I expected we'd speedily traverse the hills before us. Once we were beneath the trees, we were out of the wind. A polite dusting of snow managed to obscure landmarks and I had to trust Daro to know the way.

I amused myself thinking of how we might look to a passersby. Daro looked the part of a medieval knight astride his charger. I played the part of a princess, with my long coat draping down over the horse's hindquarters. We jogged forward through the crystalline forest, leaving clear hoof prints in the fresh snow.

For a long space of time, I forgot the serious nature of our quest. I forgot I wasn't wanted. We rode along in a dream world.

On occasion, the mare turned here or there of her

own accord and I suppose she somehow knew to avoid rough going or objects in her path. I never saw or heard Daro urge her, yet she kept going at a great, even eager pace.

"I think Ainslee-mare wants to see the top of the hills as much as we do."

Daro waved easterly. "She'll want to go until we meet the eastern trail. She'll be passing the way to her own home and birth place, the herd there at Cotton's Farm."

The trees grouped closer and closer as we traveled. I grew used to the steady thump and jounce and disregarded it, as one stops noticing the up-down of a boat of the sea.

Until the jouncing itself stopped. Abruptly, Ainslee-mare planted her huge hooves. Daro clucked and the mare angled around to point her nose toward due east.

"The way home." Daro pulled her to face northward and she again angled around. We did a little circle dance, right there, without making any forward progress.

"She knows where we are, at any rate. She wants to turn for Cotton's." Daro swung his leg up over her neck and dropped lightly to the ground. "Stay on. I'll lead her for a bit. She'll get over it, once we are away from this spot. We cannot blame her for wanting to go home!"

He took a bearing from his compass and aimed us straight into the trees. I grappled for some sort of hold of the mare's mane. The trees stood shoulder-to-shoulder and we seemed to curve every which way to fit between. I forbore to point out that this simply could not be a path. I began to doubt Daro's course. How long had it been since he crossed the island?

Flurries danced around us, though little snow penetrated through the layers of tree limbs to land on the ground. What little did accumulate muffled sound, so the great horse's hooves were nearly silent. The trees, with snow-burdened limbs, doubled the dark shadow of the deep gray sky. Every once and again we'd push through branches so close snow showered down all over us.

The air felt close, and the gray day somehow, increasingly ominous.

"We're in the foothills now. Been climbing most of this hour." Daro trudged steadily. We didn't move quite as fast as when the mare had been trotting along, but Daro kept up a good pace.

"You must have played all through these hills as a child," I said.

"No. Not much." Daro dug his compass out of his pocket again. "I thought I'd remember more landmarks. It all looks different with snow on the ground."

Hardly encouraging! I hoped we weren't lost.

He noticed my expression. "I've been to Sleeper's Falls. I'm pretty sure I can get us right there. After that, I'm not as sure, but north and west will get us to the cove."

Snow dusted all the evergreen branches. Tiny tracks, here and there, suggested squirrels were plentiful. We might have been off on a bit of a lark, and afternoon's ride to see the view.

Except it wasn't an afternoon, was it? Twilight was nearly upon us. We jolted along for ages, as the trail dwindled and trees blocked any view. I wondered if we would ever make our way to the northern coast.

Ahead, a granite-topped hill, gray against the mostly-gray sky, emerged as we cleared the thickest of the pines.

Daro paused. "It seems a world from fairytales, to me. Look at all that sky."

"It's night and day to our little coast, isn't it?" It suddenly seemed as if we had crossed into a different land. We had left behind all the charm, the pretty beaches and dunes as well as the civilized little lanes and well-kept gardens.

The interior of Cape Breton Island filled one with something more like awe. We walked out on the vertebrae of these great hills and felt the bones of them shake every time distant waves crashed violently into them. I had no words to describe the spirit roaring up from these craggy stones. Trees, twisted from constant wind, struggled upward, sparse and patchy, wherever roots could find a bit of earth.

"I cannot imagine growing up here. This forest is wild."

"I grew up far off." He must have realized how sad he sounded. "I didn't have it bad, mind. I was proud to help the family. My younger brother got schooling and all. Would have been different if I hadn't got work."

"Your younger brother, who's gone off to war?"

"Yes. He joined early. He wanted to do his part."

"You came back here, though."

He nodded slowly. "Seems like there might be a way for me to do my part, from here."

"And you take care of your mother."

"I thought I'd get a crew spot on a fishing boat, but captains hire local fellows. I do all right, though.

Deliveries, loading and unloading, anything. I earn enough."

"It's not been easy," I said it thoughtlessly, thinking more of the boy he had been, sent off when he was so young he had little memory of his home.

He turned those unfathomable dark eyes on me for a long moment. "Easy? The road before is not easy. Before you, I mean. Yet, you have set your feet upon this path." *Upon this path*...his words sounded straight from a poem and suggested many meanings.

I had chosen the path. Indeed, I had chosen my path.

"It's for good reason, this path we're following," I reminded him, finally.

I thought perhaps he hadn't heard, but no, after a pause, he began to recite small pieces of an old old poem. *"The ship... In the gales of the equinox went ashore. Into the teeth of death she sped (May God forgive the hands that fed, The false lights over the rocky Head!) Down swooped the wreckers, like birds of prey..."*

A chill raced up my spine.

"It's a horror, what they are about," he said.

"What poem is that?"

"Whittier's *The Palatine*. It's a long one. I don't recall many verses. I can almost see it, though. A great ship grounded not far from the beach, and all these men, men like vultures, waiting to rob its cargo."

It took no effort of the imagination for me to picture those folks in the holds; children nestled below decks on a ship tricked into turning into the shallows. Rocks would shatter the vessel's great timbers and freezing water would pour in. I suppressed a shudder.

At length, we clambered off the crest of rock we'd so long followed and eased down into a narrow path through dense forest. "Inland?"

"The coast is pretty rugged." I couldn't help but think our current path pretty rugged. The trees grew impossibly close. I clung to Ainslee's mane with both hands.

The trees sprouted anywhere, here and there, with barely space enough between them for the mare to squeak through. Daro turned this way and that through the maze of evergreens, ducking under or pushing aside branches and striding on.

"This is not a path." One branch caught poor Ainslee a swipe across the ears and the next swept me right off, over her backside and onto the ground.

"Captain!"

Daro grabbed my arms and hauled me to my feet before I could properly register I had hit the ground.

"Stupid of me."

"My fault entirely," I spluttered. "Might have ducked." Fortunately the deeper snow here had softened my landing. I brushed off my backside. "I could barely hang on anyway. We should lead her."

"We'll leave her. The trail beyond this is steep, and she barely fits between these tree trunks, now."

"Leave her!"

"Yes. Don't worry. She will trot straight back to Cotton's." Daro pointed the mare back downhill and removed her bridle.

The mare, freed, hovered indecisively beside us. She expected to be tacked up again, ordered, directed; such was her life. She arched her neck and nibbled at my hand, waiting, asking for a treat.

Daro waved and clucked at her. "Chick chick. Go on."

She stepped aside, took a few hesitant steps down the hill and paused, looking over her shoulder at us.

"She'll take herself along," he said. As he rolled her blanket and added it to his pack, she took a few more steps away, then a few more. She dropped her head as if to find grazing, then suddenly broke into a shambling trot. In seconds, she disappeared through the trees and away.

I could not help gazing after the big mare. "All those days she stood at the end of her paddock, staring north. She was wanting home, wasn't she? Cottons' farm and the other Clydesdales."

She'd worked for us all the summer, and in between, stood a vigil as loyal as a Mrs. Trumbull, or a Madame Chatillon. "Three grand old ladies, unable to escape their fate, but only to stand and wait." I hardly knew I had spoken aloud.

Softly, Daro said, "She's going home now, Captain."

I could only nod, as I imagined the desperate longing that bound all three to their hopes. I had no words for it, but perhaps should not be surprised the poet beside me did.

"The heart wants what it will." He touched my fingertips. "We both chose this path."

There were too many meanings in his words. I could only nod. How could I tell him how my heart had been lost weeks and weeks ago? Or, that I was not one to stand wait, and so found myself here, exhausted and freezing. In my heart, I knew I hadn't set off on this adventure to rescue people I didn't even know. No, I came simply for the chance to accompany Daro. I clung to the hope of a few more days turning into a future together.

I followed him in silence. Practicalities took over. We plunged on through the maze of trees, climbing ever upward. My legs felt the climb. I was neither used to riding for most of a day nor to hiking hillsides.

Daro swept back a snow-laden hemlock bough and I stepped into a wide, glittering expanse surrounded by crystal-coated evergreens. It might have been a glittering ballroom, so perfect and beautiful did it look. The very first time I had set eyes on Daro Michelson had been in Oceanside's vast ballroom. I stopped to gaze up the center aisle between the magnificent trees and felt myself transported back in time.

It had been the mid-summer's eve party; the night of Genevieve's grand Shakespearean ball. I could almost see the ballroom in front of me, in the beauty of the crystalline forest. I swept forward as if I still wore my long, trailing veil, only this time, I strode along beside the man of my dreams.

Our endless march through the snow continued, but I scarcely noticed.

The boring parts of party preparation and planning had fallen to me. I ordered the food, made the arrangements for the banquet hall, and made the staff assignments. I had wished that I had a less down-to-earth role, especially when I overhead all the other gals setting up the details of their 'Shakespearean event.' Oh, they had such fun with their plans. I was the working girl of the group though, so had no room to complain.

The idea for the party came too late for them to

order all-new gowns, but they certainly ordered every type of accessory and embellishment ever known and further, started recommending items for some of the gents, particularly for Avery. They'd selected him to 'play' the role of Lysander and he needed to be set apart from the more ordinary gentlemen.

They had a white wooden archway constructed inside the dining hall and a gaggle of them decorated it with flowers and twirls of tulle. On the morning of the party they had skipped around with streamers of white silk and satin. They argued over the placement of flowers as if going over battlefield tactics. The main hall became a forest of flowers.

I wanted to admire it but hadn't a moment.

I was in the midst of wrestling a huge saddle of mutton out of the oven for Cook (as the center piece of the evening meal) and listening to her mutter on about the soufflé (one of the few things she lacked confidence about cooking) and was trying to remember the small items one would expect, when Beryl asked about where to direct yet another delivery.

I rushed out, my face still beet-red from the oven.

Prince Charming emerged from the forest of flowers. Truly, the handsomest man in all the world stood before me. He swung wide the doors for me and stepped back politely. I might have been the grandest of ladies. I forgot my red face and wild hair and grubby apron.

The man offered a hand and I stepped forward and placed my fingers in the palm of his hand. He might have been a bit startled, but I smiled up at him and my heart felt near to bursting.

My prince had been him, Daro, though I didn't

know his name back then. He looked at me as though I belonged in a ballroom, as if I were the princess in this magical world. Suddenly, all of it, grand ballroom, the satins and ruffles and bunches of flowers, were for me. My prince, my party; my dream. I had stumbled into a fairytale.

For a long moment, I had believed.

"Aren't you attending the party?" Mark DeLaMore had barged up beside us. "Is everything ready for the musicians to come in?" The marvelous illusion and my wonderful prince had faded off without a word.

I glanced over at Daro, wondering if he recalled our first meeting. The summer's ball had been much of what I expected, though seeing Daro—not even properly meeting him, but seeing him—had changed everything, for always. I trudged on in his wake, with this very different, snowy enchantment all around me. The night of the ball had changed my life, and in fact, was how I had ended up on the *Thistle,* and then, here.

The party had gone on, exactly as one would expect. Yet, looking back, other little details came to light. I wished I had paid more attention at the time.

Ariel had chased after me, insisting I attend. "Elizabeth, why are you still in a day dress? I told, you, I need you as one of our forest fairies." She shoved a long trailing veil into my hands and practically pushed me up the stairs. Pushed me? No, I had floated up the stairs. Nothing else mattered. I had found the man of my dreams.

I had turned over the glittering veil in my hands. So splendid! I had become the princess. Surely, my prince awaited?

I had waltzed back down the stairs as an elegant

guest, caught up in my own dreaming.

The ballroom, filled now with people, was utterly awash with color. They say people dressed less extravagantly these days, deference to the war and all that, but apparently 'deference' did not affect this parties finery. The younger crowd wore their best; mostly off-the shoulder gowns with pearls the preferred jewelry. Most gals were rather light on 'fussy detail' as was the trend, but still with miles of fluttery, flowing fabrics. Older ladies kept to their rather more Victorian gowns, with an assortment of lacey frills. Gentlemen were black-tie, of course.

I gaped as the tide of color, scent, and sound filled every bit of space in the great hall. I distinctly recalled looking over the sea of people for Him. Oh, I knew. The man with those dark, wise eyes would not be out on a dance floor. Still, in the midst of all those colors, I had let myself hope for one more bit of magic.

Beryl had peeked from a crack in the foyer door and I had waved at her. She blushed scarlet and pressed her hands over her mouth. She was tinkled pink I'd noticed her.

Avery had popped up at my elbow. "She wanted me to wear ribbons on my wrists. Can you believe it?" He bugged his eyes, and I giggled.

Mark was hard on his heels. "I'll walk you in." He offered me an elbow and I smiled too brightly and took it. My own prince had gone.

Oh, silly as I was, I had known Daro wasn't one of the swells. I knew he wouldn't be attending the party. Perhaps I wanted anything to be possible. I had had my fair share of the practical, certainly.

"Your scene is right the end." Ariel barreled over

as Mark escorted me through the door. "We'll do the three scenes and then all the fairies move in to get everyone on the dance floor. You hang out with the spectators until I say 'All fairies.' Where is my first troop?" Doraleah and her whole gaggle lined up to follow Ariel, giggling and honking in a mad array of pastels. They all had tulle veils streaming wildly from their hair.

Madame Chatillon stood with her back to an ornate faux Grecian urn, beside the old professor. "So provincial. Lack of fashion sense. So derivative. See how all of them have the same cut, hem. Even they must dress the hair the same! I suppose it is the age."

I touched my veil (and indeed I had left my hair down.) It felt marvelous hanging loose with the veil hanging down my back. It was also exactly like everyone else's. Good grief. I could not easily change it now.

Suddenly, the Madame had given a spluttering laugh and turned aside. "Oh, the girl with no taste! No! It is too much!"

Genevieve descended the stirs so replete in embroidered and feathered and rhinestoned ensemble that she shimmered and fluttered and floated with every move. I could more easily list the fabrics and items not used than describe all those included, and how they wove together in a fascinating clash of styles, colors and sense. She might have started with a dress recalling the extremes of Victorianism, but even they had the sense not to array themselves in every bit of their finery all at once.

Madame Chatillon pressed both hands over her face and desperately tried to block her laughter. The old professor made it all worse by saying, "Why, I believe there are fish scales on her sash" with a perfectly straight face.

I myself turned and dove behind a towering vase that held a massive spray of fronds.

I have no idea how the most of the others managed good grace as Gen made her grand entrance. She pranced in, nodding and smiling in greeting with a giggly lack of dignity, perfectly sure of admiration. I suppose it stands as a credit to all the guests, (or perhaps suggested something about their own lack of fashion sense,) that no one actually collapsed in hysterical laughter.

Mrs. Brookeson, herself the height of quiet elegance in a plain slipper satin of antique blue, had smiled kindly and sent Avery a sharp nod. Avery had marched straight over to offer Gen his arm. The mid-summer's party had been the very first time he'd appeared to favor her, and most certainly had the approval of his mother.

It should have struck me as more curious, at the time. It seemed ominous, now. Had it been the first step in acquiring a new fortune?

There had been one or two other points I might have taken note of, right then. Mark had said 'Ariel ordered extra boutonnieres. Mine seems to go nicely with your gown.' I had paid him no attention, but of course, Ariel must have been in the know on my mother's matchmaking efforts and likely guessed I'd be yellow.

I had been too caught up in my own dreams. A breeze rustled through branches and brought a shimmer of sparkling snowflakes down, recalling me to exactly the non-magical place my dreams had brought me to.

Lives mattered now—peoples' lives! My daydream did me no good now…it did no one any good.

With a sinking heart, I realized my mistake. I could not help but slow Daro's progress. I should not have come. It had been entirely selfish on my part. My legs ached dreadfully but I had to go on. He'd made such an effort. The lives of a whole shipload of people might right now hang on whether or not I could keep the pace.

I shut my mind to my freezing feet and aching legs. I tried to breathe through my scarf, so I didn't take in great gasping breaths of freezing air. I would not slow the hero. What I would give for a plate of Cook's little sandwiches and large hot toddy right now! Back at mid-summer, would I have even guessed I might find myself trudging over the island on a freezing winter day? I made myself put such thoughts aside. My comfort did not matter. My feelings for Daro, likewise, had to be out aside for now. Our errand mattered so terribly!

"I can hear it now," he said at length.

I could hear nothing, in the heavy, snow-muted air of the forest. I trudged on without comment.

"We're nearly at the base of the falls. It'll be dark before long."

Base of the falls? Great stars, we were nowhere near the top of our climb, yet. We strode on to a small cairn marked the end of our trail. Years of hikers' footprints lead to overlook the falls, and I stumbled there for a glimpse. A narrow chasm cut a plumb line down between the trees. The far bank was steeply undercut, and the water streamed by several feet below the top of the bank. Tendrils of ice hugged the edges, but still an enormous amount of water rushed passed.

"Don't go near the edge." Daro unslung his pack and carefully unwrapped his thermos. "From here, it's a hard climb."

From here? I could only stand and stare.

The hills rolled straight down into the sea. Plumes of fog twisted up from white capped waves and rounded snow-covered hills dropped abruptly into the sea. Even in the fading light, I could see the shore trail weaving its way northward.

"Our artist would paint this view, and nothing else, if once he set eyes on this place." Snow covered everything. There was not one dry spot to rest, no handy stump or rock, or one square foot of dry land.

"Trouble Cove is north of Pleasant Bay. We'll have good views of all the shore along here."

"We won't be able to see anything much longer." Although all day had been chilly, gray and overcast, I could sense the deepening dark and feel the sun disappearing over some hidden horizon. "Will we find shelter under the trees?"

He did not look at me, but pulled out his compass and studied it in silence. Finally, he said, "We may not be in time, if we stop. "

"What?"

He pulled a metal cookie tin from his pack, the sort you get on Christmas morn, and opened it to reveal an array of small items. He selected a matchbook, one match, and carefully tucked away the cookie tin. Next, he pulled a black metal lantern from his pack.

He lifted the mantle with extraordinary care to light the lantern. "This is a miner's light," he explained as he fixed the catch. "It works like a lighthouse beacon, on a gas, and shines forward from the mirror behind the glass."

"It's bright enough." The light sent a sure white beam straight ahead.

We would travel through the night? All I could think of was rest. I know it was weak of me, but my legs wanted to stop. I leaned against a particularly large pine, a cold cold pine, and wished I could sit. I had expected we would stop after all this long way. I'd dragged myself along this whole last hour thinking, 'night is coming, night is coming.'

I took a sip of the lukewarm tea Beryl had packed for us. Why had I insisted on coming along? My efforts were useless. Couldn't change it now. "Right. Lead on then," I made myself say. I would have to force myself to follow, somehow.

"Been thinking about Mrs. Buxton's meat pie in here, this whole last hour or more. I guess we can stop long enough for a bite?"

He was asking me? I nodded and allowed my head to lean against the handy tree trunk. I heard him digging around in the pack, heard the voice in the creak of the ancient tree.

Daro handed me a square of meat pie. Mrs. Buxton had been our cook all summer long, and I could not recall ever tasting a dish finer than her meat pie. The pie or the tree or Daro's encouragement worked. My legs stopped aching as I recalled our purpose.

We left the edge of the waterfall and marched upward through the thin layer of fresh snow. As the trees grew sparser, the snow grew deeper, until we struggled through thigh-deep drifts in places. The dreamy rest stop became memory too quickly.

Daro broke through the top crust of the snow. I

struggled to step into his footprints rather than break through myself. My woolen tights were no match for the snow.

The minor's light lit our way forward with an odd, luminescent glow.

Thin, wind-twisted trees offered no cover as we struggled yet higher, however, as the hill grew steeper and steeper, there was less snow. Soon, we clambered over little more than bare rock. Thankfully, it was great slabs of granite, solid and unmoving. No loose rocks slipped or tumbled as we made our way upward, and the handholds were secure.

The unforgiving cold took its toll. Even with the thick boiled wool mittens over my ladies' gloves, my fingers went numb. I wore the edges of my everyday boots to tatters. Daro's fancy minor's lantern, fixed to a sturdy helmet, lit his way better than mine. I did the best I could to follow his path exactly, but I at times I almost had to feel my way along.

A long time after we left the waterfall behind, and at a point where I had ceased to think anything at all, I glanced up to try to aim for Daro's next foothold, and something glittered in the sky above. Actually, quite a lot of things glittered, and I stood a long moment puzzled, too tired to think clearly, before I realized the skies had cleared and we could see the stars.

A finer chandelier I have never seen.

"Stars," I called to Daro, as if he wouldn't have noticed. "A gift."

"Stars," he repeated. He swung around to look at me. "Your brightness is a gift to me, Captain. You buoy my spirits more than the light of the heavens."

Again, he spoke the words the way he quoted

poems. I guessed he'd been thinking up those lines as he walked. As he turned away, he said, "What price the light?"

He didn't mean for me to hear and once, I'd have been gracious and pretended I hadn't. I put aside such courtesy and said outright, "I don't understand."

"Captain…I ask myself every day if I cannot take up a normal life. I can hardly ask you to follow a wanderer."

Before I could reply he jerked his head northward. "There's no time. It's taking us too long."

Chapter Thirteen
A Way with Light

The steepest stretch gave way to a flat-topped granite plateau. Two great standing stones jutted skyward from the rough center. Scrawny trees with sparse branches sprouted stubbornly through every crack, but no creatures moved. In the hazy pre-dawn light before sunrise, we could make out little more than shadows.

"The island's blue stones." Daro nodded to the pair. "For good fortune."

"Good fortune," I repeated as we strode by them. We paused at the northern edge of the plateau. The steep green hillside slid down into clouds of fog and we could make out the sea only in patches.

"This lookout is almost legendary." Daro raised binoculars but didn't scan the sea. Rather, he studied the very edge of the coast. I couldn't guess what he hoped to see. Night had barely faded. The fog obscured all but the vaguest detail. To the south, the fog had thinned to thin skeins as if etched by an artist's brush.

"Trouble Cove is supposed to be a half-moon shape." He swept the binoculars along the most northern coast.

"Supposed to be?"

"I've only seen it on maps. We should be almost above it."

I looked straight down. Below, a perfect crescent carved out the edge of the coastline. The top of the crescent ended in shallow shoals, while the lower end curved out to sea.

A dot of light shone from the center of the beach. As I stared, I could make out the busy-bee shapes of men as they fed a fire. A flash revealed the presence of a mirror. I seized Daro's arm and pointed.

"It's true," I hissed, still not quite believing. "They are directing the light out to sea, imitating a lighthouse!"

"And there are the lights of a ship!" I followed the direction of his binoculars. Faintly, a row of lights glimmered from distant waves.

"It looks like she's already turning. It's a big one." Daro dropped the binoculars and stared below with eyes full of horror. "We are too late."

"If only the fog would clear. If only the sailors could see shore."

Daro waved his hand toward the eastern horizon. "Sun will be up in a minute, but it won't clear the fog fast enough for the ship's crew to see their danger. We are too far to warn them!"

No plan or effort of ours would change anything now. We would be only silent watchers to this horrendous, cruel act.

"There might be children aboard." Daro stood in the midst of the rock plateau, shaking with rage and helplessness. He lifted binoculars again. "She's making slow headway. If only we could douse the false light. If only one of those men had a conscience."

"An hour's climb down," I said, desperately. "There's no way to reach them. If only it were light."

"Light." Daro swung round east. The standing stones, behind us, caught his attention. "The Sun. Quick! The fogbank—our canvas!" Daro ran to the standing stones, but the threshold of the stone monoliths sat well above his head.

I scurried after him, confused.

"Between the stones, between the standing stones." He motioned wildly so I followed him to the foot of the great rocks. Without hesitation he hoisted me up into the gap between the two.

The first true rays of sunlight burst over the eastern horizon as I straightened. A river of light poured around me and shone out to sea.

The stone monoliths channeled the light, throwing my shadow against the glittering, brightly lit fogbank.

An enormous specter rose up above the beach. Startled, I flung my arms wide and the giant, likewise, flung its arms out. I know I gasped. Daro gasped. To the men, it must have seemed a giant figure emerged from the fog itself and stood over them.

From far, far below, we heard screams and then shouting as the figures ran away from the bonfire. The men dispersed in all directions.

Perhaps those on the ship saw the glittering giant as well. More likely, they became alert when their guide light stopped. Without the man focusing the mirror in imitation of a lighthouse, the flash that signified a lighthouse beacon stopped, leaving only the odd flicker of flames on the beach.

The ship's progress slowed. After a few minutes, we could see by the change in the angle of the lights she had turned. The ship eased northward and avoided the waiting rocky shoals. It had taken only a moment's interruption for them to realize it had not been a true navigational light. I watched the ship lights so carefully, I didn't notice the giant's shadow sink away before the sun's rays.

The giant being of light, crafted by one who knew the sky, had saved them all.

Daro shouted the triumphant words of Wordworth, "in the vastness of Being..." as he rushed to me. I plunged down into his waiting arms and twirled there, my feet not even touching the ground.

Finally, laughing, I asked, "Whatever did it look like to those at the foot of the shimmering giant shadow?"

"Like The Almighty himself stood witness to their crime! They ran, they all ran!" Daro gently set me on my feet, laughing.

I can hardly describe my emotion. Too much happened in the space of seconds. Daro's understanding of light and atmosphere had given us this one weapon: Fear.

The men had scattered, most of them southward. They had left dories on the beach and departed as if truly terrified. The quality of the light changed. Sunlight chased away the fog.

One form still ran about the beach, gesticulating. The ring leader I guessed. Avery? It was too far to tell. He'd not be frightened off by a trick of the light, but it was too late for him to change anything. His trick had failed and the big ship has escaped his snare.

"A glory on cloud bank," Daro explained. "When I saw the direction of the standing stones, I guessed they were set to channel the dawn's light. Some ancient builder saved that ship today."

"The ship is safe, isn't it?" I leaned forward, gazing north. "How did you ever know?"

"I can hardly believe it worked." Daro clasped his hands together and stared heavenward. I too, could only think to send thanks. How long we stood, there on this great granite crest between sea and sky, I can hardly tell.

We stood hand-in-hand. And, I thought to give my thanks right then for him, as well all the events of our day.

Chapter Fourteen
The Lighthouse

Unbelievably, we were not done. I stumbled down the path after Daro, though I could not guess what more we could accomplish. Avery's chance was gone. He would have to wait weeks for the right combination of approaching ship and poor light conditions. I would make darn sure he never got ahold of those letters with the ship schedules, again.

"Perhaps we should go back?" I called. "We can warn everyone. He'll not get another chance!"

Daro strode straight down the slope at impossible speed. "This was no less than attempted murder. You're right he'll never get another chance. We'll not just be hoping. We'll stop him for good."

A chill touched me as he spoke. My Daro aimed to make an end to it, at whatever cost.

The north face of the granite hills was steeper and shorter than the southern side. A plain path ran down between the scraggily trees, and loose rocks made it treacherous in a different way from our climb up. I fell behind.

Daro made it to the beach first and did not wait. No telling when the group of men might return. Alone, even he was no match for all those we had seen on the beach. I had to reason with Daro. I scurried out onto the beach in time to see Daro charge like a bull at someone coming along from the keeper's cottage. The someone, as I had expected, looked tall and thin. Avery.

Avery plunged forward with unusual bravado. I glanced all around, sure someone must be about to help him. He would never challenge someone the size of Daro. Still, I saw no one and suspected something worse; he had a weapon of some kind.

I grabbed up an abandoned oar from the beach and ran headlong toward the two men. They'd stopped within inches of one another. Avery yanked out a long, wicked-looking knife. Daro angled around, as if ready to tackle him, risking being cut.

I barreled straight at them, swung my oar violently at Avery and—though I did not connect—Avery let out a gasping scream, jerked back and allowed the knife to fall to the sands. He must have recalled the unfortunate moment when he met the business end of my fireplace poker.

Daro plowed straight into him and knocked him down.

"No," someone screeched. "No, no, no!" I saw I had been right about Genevieve, as well. Still far off, she came scrambling down the wooden walkway from the cottage. "Stop, stop."

Avery curled up in a ball, refusing to get up.

Daro kicked over remnants of bonfire on the beach, and grabbed the mirror they had mounted on a crate. In one swift motion, he smashed it. "Murderer! The false light." He shook the crate at Avery's head. "You could have killed people."

"Stop!" Gen came racing across the beach, her winter furs flowing out like some sort of ancient warrior princess. She was gorgeous and beautiful and I could not imagine how she could have been party to this horror.

What had she imagined? This ship would have turned too early and crashed onto the treacherous shoals well south of the real, northernmost lighthouse. The vessel and people and all a manner of goods would have been plunging in the waves, while men went out to retrieve items of value. Had she known? How could she not?

How could she ignore the Trouble Cove lighthouse, far out on the point, burnt into a blackened shell?

Seeing the remnants of the light, I recalled there should have been a lighthouse keeper. Poor man, I hadn't even given the keeper a thought. Avery's group must have prevented him from protecting the light.

Daro grabbed Avery's elbow and hauled him to his feet.

Genevieve thundered up to us. "What do you think you are doing? We'll report you to the police!"

Daro stared down at her then turned to look at me.

"And explain about causing a shipwreck?" I snapped as I stepped in between them.

"You don't understand! It's our patriotic duty! We're out here to help the war effort. We are tricking the enemy submarines!" She smacked her hand into the back of her palm. "Avery is a hero, don't you see?"

Daro snorted.

Genevieve only then thought to look around. "Where are all the volunteers?"

"Volunteers? Genevieve, those men were out here to wreck and rob a passenger ship."

Genevieve dismissed my words. She clutched

Avery's arm and chattered along about how we didn't understand. She sported a sparkling engagement ring and clung to him like she had found her dream. How sad for poor Gen.

Avery, in a phony, soft voice, said, "I told you to stay in the cottage, my dear. It could be dangerous."

Dangerous! I thought of the men on the beach. Some of them might not have gone all that far. They'd left so quickly, they had left behind all their supplies. Indeed, dories still sat on the sand, along with hand-carts and empty crates and all a manner of items.

Tire prints marked where the Packard had turned and retreated. Osten? Oh, it was simply a nightmare to contemplate who else might be involved. The manager might have assisted Avery, and maybe some of the other men. I worried that silly Mark DeLaMore might have followed his cousin into this horror, to say nothing of the other society boys.

Daro stood looking down at the couple, his face unreadable. He could certainly beat the hell out of Avery, but he'd no idea what to with Gen. For that matter, what could we really do with Avery? We were miles from any authority we might turn him in to. I looked around the beach. The ship was safely away—there was only our word for what he had been up to.

Avery clutched his jaw with one hand and leaned toward Gen.

"What is wrong with you?" she scolded Daro.

Daro looked at me again.

"That was a passenger ship out there, Gen," I repeated.

"Nonsense." She patted Avery's back and glared at me. "You're horrible—disgraceful, that's what you are!

Out here wandering around with, with the delivery man!"

"Gen, aren't you here alone with Avery?"

"Of course not! At least, we were escorted by several gentlemen until they all ran off. I can't imagine what happened."

"Submarine targeted the beach. Panicked our patriotic crew." Avery jerked his head to us. "You can't reason with them. They have no any idea of how difficult it is to protect Canada."

"Attacking you! And only to cover up their own bad behavior." She caught Avery under the arm to help him along.

Avery, still holding his face with one hand, smirked. "No one will believe a word you say."

Daro took one step forward. Both of them staggered back.

"I know what you were about here." Daro stared straight into Avery's face. "I don't need anyone to believe me. I could throw you straight off the cliff face onto the rocks and watch the gulls rip your innards out, piece by piece."

Genevieve, as pale as the snow itself, gaped. Avery, pale as a ghost, grimly kept a grip on her arm.

"If I catch you at it again, it'll be a cliff for you. Understand?"

Avery kept backing away. "We'll call this a misunderstanding. We'll go, we'll leave it all alone."

Genevieve sneered at me. "Aren't you ashamed?"

The two of them walked slowly away from us and then toward the coast road in the chilly morning light.

"Those men," I wondered aloud.

"Gone, I'd say." Daro scanned the edges of the

forest. "Even if they aren't afraid to return to the beach, they're probably afraid to return and face Avery."

I hadn't thought of that.

Daro touched my shoulder, soft as a sea breeze. "I'm glad you sailed with me again, Captain."

"The keeper?"

He plainly had not thought of the man, either. He stumbled off toward the keeper's cottage. He felt tired and sore, I guessed, beyond all the imagining.

After all the events of the day, it was hard to believe it was little more than morning. We had done it, after all. I, exhausted beyond all measure myself, went to sit on a sun-warmed rock left high and dry by the retreating tide. Two fair-sized crab picked around a shallow tidal pond at my feet. A third scuttled around a bit of a puddle.

After a while, Daro sank down in the sand beside me and hunched forward, eyes half-closed against the sun's glare. "I could not find the keeper. He's the only one who might have backed up our claims."

"What about those other men? Did you recognize anyone?"

"None of them were locals. No one from around here would have thought anything about the odd effects of light on fog." Daro leaned heavily against the granite boulder. "No islander would have run off in a panic because of a reflection."

"It startled me," I admitted.

"I think I shall never forget the blue glow around you, casting a spectral form out onto the bank of fog." Daro stared out over the open ocean, as if the strange form might conjure up before us again. "Not one witness will ever forget."

I wanted to ask what came next, if we should pursue the other men we had seen, or if we might somehow replace the lighthouse's beacon. I could not bring myself to trouble his rest, and remained silent, thinking of the long, long road home.

Some hours before the turn of the tide, Daro and I sat cross-legged in the sand and cooked crab in the remnants of the bonfire. I think I have never tasted anything so fine.

At last, we set off on the long walk toward McLellan's Harbor. The fog lifted as the sea breeze came up. Daro offered me his arm. "I gave no thought to the return trip."

Nor had I—nor had I. We had run off to save the world and hadn't given the return a thought. We began to walk. We strolled over the beach sands and went by the long crescent of rock ledge that held the keeper's cottage, poised on a spit of land to the south.

I paused. "The true light is ruined. It's a danger, isn't it? No navigational light."

"I'll report it to coastal patrol. I'll worry about the keeper, though."

I feared he had met some terrible harm, and at the same time, I couldn't help walking out on the spit of land, toward the keeper's cottage.

"Wouldn't it be magical to live right here, with a view out over the sea? It would almost be like living on board a ship, with waves right at your feet."

"Live here," he repeated. "So far? No neighbors, no stores?"

"It is near enough to visit." I eased around the cottage for the eastern view. Our artist might never tire of this one place, had he but the chance to see it. White crested waves curled into a jagged rock barely yards from the shore. I eased around the building and southward, looking not over beach sands, but over a grassy bluff that plunged directly down to the sea.

I waved at the magnificence before us. "There is a different view from every window of this cottage."

A call answered my words at once. "Help!"

I think we both jumped.

"The well!" Daro ran forward, calling as he went.

The voice answered, croaking out 'help' again and again, until Daro suddenly shouted, "Donnall! Is that you?"

It took man minutes to find rope and urge Donn to tie himself in and for us to find some point of leverage, but at last, Daro had his friend safely up and out of the well.

We were a long time getting ready to go, after that. Poor Donnall had been thrown down the well by the gang and had been scarcely able to keep above the frigid waters. Until he heard our voices, he had no idea the huge group of men had departed.

To think he might not have called out, if we hadn't wandered around the little cottage, instead of taking the road! Sheer chance brought us close to the keeper's cottage and its fresh water well.

Once Donn seemed able, we set off south. Poor Donnall! His temporary job had nearly killed him. I hoped poor Alma wouldn't think of that. At least we would get him home, assuming we managed to get ourselves there.

We followed the road inland, hopeful despite the distance.

All at once, Daro turned around and pointed to the

keeper's charming dwelling. "What you said, about the lighthouse cottage? Did you mean it...truly?"

"It would be like living on a ship, wouldn't it? With waves crashing right at the doorstep. Like the day aboard the *Thistle*. I have so often wished our sail never ended."

He strode head-down with the silhouette of the rocky hill face behind him. He might have been made of the same granite. He didn't look at me, but began speaking in a low, flat voice, filled with doom. "I wanted to be free. I want to look at the sky whenever I want."

I could only trot after him, wondering what he meant.

"Captain, you've been a good friend, but meant so much more. I've been afraid. Afraid I can't be good enough to be the sort of man..." he broke off.

The blue of sky and sea swirled together through my mist of tears as I stumbled on. I could not let him see, as I struggle with my heart heavy and nothing before me but the road.

"Fact is, I can hardly imagine a better life than a lighthouse keeper." He stomped even faster. "Fact is, I cannot imagine you leaving."

I still scurried, fairly panting, as I said, "Well it's a beautiful spot..." Wait. What?

"I expected Oceanside to shut its doors and you'd go back to city and society, where you came from. I could resign myself to it. I steeled myself for it. I told myself it would be a relief."

He motioned toward the sea. "For myself, I could never return to city life, or working indoors, or hearing doors slam to shut me in.

"But I could live at a lighthouse." He did not look at me, this man who had charged the enemy, climbed through the granite hills and somehow used the magic of light, itself, to save a thousand lives.

"A lighthouse would be like living on the sea itself, with the wilds and waves all around." I put one hand on his arm.

He hung his head. "You're sure you would not pine for fine city life?"

I caught his hand. It was enough for me, but the poet in him would not be stilled.

He caught both my hands and said, "No cloud dare mar the skies as I dream of your bright eyes."

I knew enough not to cast about for this quote, for these were his own words and composed for me.

We walked on, until, lo and behold, here came George, puttering along in the finest of Russell Motorcars.

Could I live in a lighthouse!

Chapter Fifteen
Accusations

A proper poem or any self-respecting tale would end right there; in the heartfelt moment with a nod to the future, but my story, our story now, carried forward on a most insistent current. Though we'd braved the high seas, a few waves awaited.

George, as it happened, had been sent by the very worried Alma, who had heard bits and pieces of our plans from Beryl. George, with the best of intentions, brought us to Oceanside's front door.

We were met with varying levels on consternation.

"Utter disgrace." Mrs. Brookeson reeled theatrically away as she turned us from the front door. She wouldn't hear any argument. "Roaming all over forests and beaches with some rough local man, unescorted, overnight. Interrupting a brave, patriotic plan!"

I crept back from the hotel's front stairs, telling myself I had no need to feel shame, but embarrassed and angry nonetheless.

Donnall spoke up. "Instead of accusing these two, we ought to be calling them heroes."

I was glad he spoke, but still, I trembled to think about Mrs. Brookeson's accusations. What would society think of me? Never mind society, what would my parents say?

"Heroes." Madame Chatillon descended the stair toward Donnall. "Heroes?"

"They saved a passenger ship heading for port from wrecking." Donnall pointed dramatically toward the sea, before continuing. "Me, as well. I'd have frozen to death, if I'd not got help."

"Nothing to do with anything," Mrs. Brookeson snapped. I stood there, wanting to argue but knowing—knowing—we had saved the ship. I could argue the point, and yet, here I was, in the same place I had been. Hero or not, my parents would still not approve of Daro.

The argument raged on, but I hardly heard.

Daro caught my hand, made a face, and suddenly, none of it mattered. We'd stopped the awful crime. People could think what they liked.

George, one foot on his running board, called, "We ought to give Daro the keep of the Trouble Cove light. He'd do double duty as keeper and coastal watcher. I intend to speak to the coast patrol."

Bigger waves followed, as you'd guess. The tide carried in a lot of changes. Donnall's testimony alongside ours got the Brookesons investigated. The curtain closed on Oceanside.

Mrs. Trumbull opened a Bed and Breakfast. Oceanside's remaining guests, including the just-arrived Madame Chatillon's grandson, became her first guests. Beryl went on up there too, to do for Mrs. Trumbull's guests.

Ariel, practical to a fault, hustled her sister home to Halifax, but Gen easily weathered the changing tide and floated right back into the Halifax social scene.

Funny how things turned out. George did indeed

convince the town to award the lighthouse keeper's duty to Daro. The lighthouse made all the difference to me…as that final wave carried the two of us to the church. For my part, I think had been swept away from the day I had first set foot on the little sailboat, *Thistle*.

Epilogue
Christmas at the Cove

The morning of Christmas Eve arrived like a scene from the old artist's brush. It might be framed somewhat differently from the rest of my story, but it mirrored real life well-enough. White-capped waves splashed onto snowy rocks while the diamond glitter of stars swirled about the sky. The island was as it always was, yet so much had changed...although not for each of us. I floated into a dream on the arm of my prince charming, almost oblivious to other's stories...

Patrick strolled into the kitchen of the lighthouse keeper's cottage and settled into the chair by the window. "You've changed your hair."

Alysa, who was not Alysa at all, but he knew her only by her assumed name, blushed as she patted the edge of her soft new bob. It was the latest—a wild shot at copying the looks she'd seen in the ladies magazines from oversees. "Almost sunrise," she murmured. *A predawn riser, like me.*

"Best of the day," he asserted. "The morning twilight makes the ocean's depths darker and the crest of each wave all the whiter."

"The sky is as often as beautiful as the ocean here." Alysa set a tray of scones on the table and went to stand by the window, as well.

"Yes." Patrick waved his hand toward the sky.

"I've studied light, controlling light, worked on strengthening beams of light and yet, here among these strange clouds and fogs, I find I am constantly amazed by the light."

"I am afraid I've simply admired it." Alysa felt completely tongue-tied. Could this be it? Magic could happen at Christmas-time, surely, if ever it could. She clasped her hands and tried to focus. She must somehow manage to keep up a conversation with this most learned man!

"Indeed, light is worth study. These low clouds filter light in something of a kaleidoscope effect." He gazed to the east. "I've spent such a long time, trying to improve the lens design on this new beacon to increase its reach. I wish I had thought to study the sky."

"To warn mariners far out at sea," she said. "To save lives."

"Indeed, it is the greatest good I can imagine."

The greatest good! One could not doubt the sincerity of his warm, deep voice. A brilliant man and yet so humble! Butterflies tumbled about her insides, but she managed to say, quite ridiculously given the seriousness of his objective, "I often look for the tiny twinkling of rainbows rolling in ahead of each wave."

Patrick nodded. "The curve of the wave improves intensity in the same way we make an aperture collimate a beacon of light." His voice resonated with perfect surety. "The works of nature are there, to teach us. If we are clever enough to interpret the magnificence before us. Design of improved optical systems demands no less."

Alysa could only assume he had said something quite brilliant. "I suppose it is all a matter of atmospheric conditions and silly to see it as magical."

"I find I am utterly swept away by the magical." He extended his hand.

To me? How…amazing, impossible… She started to reach for him, in the midst of sunrise and rainbows and her heart beating louder than the crash of ocean waves.

Patrick said, "The practical applications make these conditions useful."

Practical. Useful.

She dropped her hand. *Who loves the practical?* A voice amazingly like her mother's chastised her at once. Abruptly, she spun back to the kitchen counter.

'Practical' ruined everything again!

Plainly, dear, wonderful Patrick found her eminently practical. She hadn't meant to be. She'd bobbed her hair and even brought her hemline up nigh onto an inch. She'd added two feathers to her Sunday hat and wore earrings everyday now, to be in with the fashionable. She'd talked about magic and rainbows and yet, there it was. Practical.

"Let me get this coffee on." Her words tumbled over themselves and she didn't think he had even heard. She busied herself with the dishes and held her breath to hold back tears. After a moment, she managed, in quite a normal voice, "One day, it will be wonderful to see the new lighthouse lit."

He stood up and turned from the eastern window, the sky streaked with the orange and gold of sunrise behind him. "Some things take time. Surprising time."

She refused to make a fool of herself. She refrained from rushing to his side, to assure him the light, and his design, would surely prove to be the best, most extraordinary, ever.

Practical practical practical! What had she let herself imagine? The lighthouse sat there, big and expensive and completely untried. It would be entirely fanciful to imagine it as extraordinary. It was fanciful to think its designer was anyone special, too. She would not be fanciful. He could plainly see right through her chameleon-like ensemble, and make out the plain old practical gal at the heart.

He settled at the table, but not she! She busily stoked the stove to speed the coffee along. The others trickled in and settled about the table. Dear Elizabeth almost danced into the room but she, so used to waiting on people, came right over to assist Alyssa.

"Let me take over here, Ari-, er, Alysa," Elizabeth offered.

None of the guests noticed their hostess' little slip. Alysa rolled her eyes. Elizabeth playfully clasped a hand over her mouth and slapped her forehead.

The success of her little subterfuge didn't matter much, Alyssa who was in fact Ariel had to acknowledge. She simply wanted to avoid talk...no one knew her here...fortunes and scandals simply didn't matter.

Elizabeth stood below the small painting the old hotel's old artist had made. He'd captured the wondrous day, nigh onto a year ago, when Elizabeth and her young man had strolled up to the McLellan Harbor church, arm-in-arm, moments before their vows. Vows to one another, to remain together, to never be alone again in this life...suddenly it was all too much and Alysa, choked back a sob and flew from the room.

Elizabeth scurried after her.

Determined not to make a scene, Alysa stopped by the backdoor and pretended she cared about nothing more than Elizabeth divulging her identity. "I don't know why I am worried," she said, in a plain a voice as she could manage. "It hardly matters."

"No even one noticed, Ariel. And no one would care." Elizabeth hesitated, puzzled. "Do come back in?"

"Yes, yes." They went back to the table and joined the merry chatter.

As keeper of the lighthouse, Elizabeth's husband strolled in last, having checked every inch of his domain at first light. He grinned at the small gathering. "Special holiday news. You're all invited to this evening's revelries at the village. Mrs. Trumbull's offered to put everyone up overnight, too."

He turned to Patrick. "I'll ask you to drive the ladies of the household down for the party, as I'll have to stay at my post."

"I'll stay here at the lighthouse," Alysa volunteered. Better to stay alone than continue to delude herself!

"Oh, surely not." Patrick frowned. "We should all go. Isn't one night without a keeper is acceptable? I mean, we are not even permitted to switch on the light. How much can it matter if we all go?"

The keeper shook his head. "I could alert help if we spotted a ship in trouble. And we must always keep watch for an invasion."

"Invasion." Patrick snorted. "Christmas Eve! How likely."

"Do not concern yourself on my account," the big man cut him off. "I am proud to stand my post."

"For every single day of the year," Alysa

interrupted him. "This once, you go. I am perfectly capable of watching and alerting, if it comes to it."

She brooked no argument. Elizabeth had offered to stay as well, but it would be she and her husband's first Christmas together. She was persuaded. They all were, in the end. They had all gone. Patrick had gone.

Over and over, Alysa chided herself for allowing her ridiculous imaginings. Patrick, handsome and clever, would easily meet met any young woman's criteria. Why, why would she imagine he'd wish to take up with a plain Jane? No matter how handsome or how clever, she meant, no matter how clever a man, it was neither smarts nor practicality he wanted in a woman. *I should have learned that, at least, from Mama.*

He'd departed perfectly charmingly, saying "my dear Alysa, there'll be no lightness in this evening without you." It meant nothing. He spoke pleasantly to all.

Oh, but he seemed quite sincere! *Seemed*, rang in her head, still in her mother's voice.

Alysa walked along the rock point mere feet above the sea, mindlessly watching the foaming waves.

The Trouble Cove lighthouse, a newly built, crisp white tower at the tip of Nova Scotia's northernmost island, sank into the evening's darkness. The beacon sat unlit. At sea, no ship could use her guide for their navigation, for good or ill.

Human-sounding voices called in the gusts of wind...then disappeared into the crash of waves.

"The blackout continues," Alysa muttered aloud. She meant it in a rather personal way, though of course, the 'blackout order' meant all of Canada's lighthouses sat in darkness until the end of the Great War.

Patrick, the designer of this new light, looked so devastated when they'd received word, that she had hurried to over to grasp his hand. He had surprised her with the strength of his grasp. She'd only meant to comfort, but her heart had leapt. Suddenly, hand-in-hand with Patrick, she'd somehow allowed herself to imagine all sorts of possibilities! She'd spent one whole afternoon pouring over magazines and primping as if she had a real suitor. Why ever had she even entertained the notion?

Obviously, Patrick had felt gratitude for her sympathy, nothing more. She could not be so silly as to imagine more.

She stood with the great tower to her back and stared toward the eastern stars, trying to let the sound of the crashing surf fill her mind completely. There at the foot of the freshly built, freshly painted tower, she could not but recall Patrick's desperate, "Who would guess the war would grind on so tenaciously?"

Already Christmas nineteen seventeen, yet the war overseas raged on; on and on. Canadian soldiers continued to ship overseas regularly, along with supplies, ammunition, and desperate hopes. The horror of it all seemed endless. Although far, it provided a dark backdrop for her own despair.

Another Christmas and here she was again, soul-alone. *Too practical.*

"Truly," she said aloud. "Too practical?"

Her mother had chastised her over and over—had, in fact, only recently written, *'put aside this stubborn insistence on practicality. It is not an attractive quality in a young woman! Do you wish to be alone all your life?'*

"Oh Mama, better alone than with some fool, like the one Gen is doting on right now?" Alysa could not understand why her parents did not see how plainly unsuitable her sister's latest suiter was. Alysa shook her head. A young man utterly bereft of ambition or skill! Ridiculous!

Why, any woman in their right mind would much prefer the handsome Patrick, not, oh not at all, for his crystal blue eyes and firm jaw, nor even his frank, sensible demeanor, but for his vision! He applied himself to design and create objects of value, objects like lights and guidance apparatus, to be used by many, many people.

One could not fail to admire the practical application of all he created! He'd made a model of the lighthouse beacon, no more than a tiny twinkle of a light, yet the beam reached nigh on to the first house of the nearby village. Why, a big lantern never reached so far. He planned to go on creating all sorts of useful things. He was undeniably a perfectly practical man.

Oh dear.

Perhaps her mother was right, and all thoughts of good sense and practical matters should be put aside for matters of the heart.

Except she couldn't.

Not that she hadn't hopes. After all, at Christmas, anything could happen.

Alysa sighed heavily as she placed her hand on the base of the tower. The pulse of the waves washed upward, through the rock and wood. Another howl rode in on a gust of wind. The approaching storm insisted on making itself heard.

Surely, practicality might be seen as an asset, to

some? *An asset in an assistant, or a cook, but hardly what inspired romance...*she heard the words as if in her mother's voice.

It doesn't matter, it doesn't matter at all, she assured herself, but it mattered. In spite of all her hopes, it mattered too much.

Quite alone with the night, she let herself think back over those few moments of breakfast.

Certainly, she had allowed herself to imagine it, if he had seemed extraordinarily courteous at any point? He had indeed gone along with the others for the holiday party. There would be the Christmas Eve dinner, then the church visit, then the dance. No doubt, many a young maid would be dancing with Patrick this evening—why, likely right this minute!

Alysa hunched up by the tower, the lonely, empty tower. Someday, after the war perhaps, the extraordinary reach of the new light would be proved. Opportunity lay quite beyond its own value or function, it had but to stand until called for.

She clasped a hand to her face, and no longer noticed the sound of the surf, or the wind howling with human-sounding voices. She'd had decided to stay here as watcher, and watch she would. Even without a light, someone must watch for ships in peril.

"Entirely a practical matter," she muttered. "I'm not surprised and not disappointed Patrick went with them."

She felt completely alone.

One lonely, desperate howl, as if indeed someone called from out beyond the breakers broke through the sound of the surf. For well over an hour now, she'd heard human-sounding voices. She heard them when the great pines at the foot of the hill swayed, when the seal barked to one another in the waves, and even in the quiet of the afternoon, when nothing at all explained a voice. She'd come out, in the first place, to be assured of the empty beach and quiet sea.

Still, this one, unearthly wail called out so insistently, she stopped on the stone landing beside the tower and peered into the darkness out at sea.

The wolf howl raised goosebumps on her arms. Chills ran up her spine. All at once, she found herself racing down the length of the beach calling, calling to someone who was most surely there.

"Here, I am here," she called still running, between gasps for breath. Oh surely, it was surely someone?

In the dark of night, who could tell? Her loneliness had seemed so complete, so utterly permanent when she offered to mind the lighthouse, she had no idea how she could come to feel worse. Yet, her long empty afternoon contemplating a lifetime emptiness had taught her 'worse.' Oh, she'd wish no one the harm of a sinking ship or stranding at sea, but oh, let this be someone.

A young man desperate for help, and be just the right age to be a proper suiter.

A man's voice, more clearly, called, "Help. I cannot see the shore!"

Her mind was all a muddle. A man alone, not far off the beach? This could be no foundered ship. Surely this is what she was to watch against? Unknown men invading the coast? Only one voice called!

"Helloooo," she called into the endless dark of night. She would not be surprised to hear nothing. Her mind had conjured visitors before. Still, she moved to light the small hurricane lamp at the end of the walk, and carried it hastily down to the beach. It had been a voice. A person. She did not really believe it.

She slowed to a walk as she reached the small dory. A madness, thinking someone had called.

"Help," he called, again.

There! On the rocky point of the tombolo she knew well. At low tide, you could easily wade out to the point, though a lot of water stood between rock and beach at the moment. Still, she had the spot fixed in her mind. She needed only to keep a good thought as to the direction of shore.

Without further thought, she dragged the dory down to the water.

"I'm coming," she called. The freezing water took her breath, but she needed to wade out into the waves to shove off. The arc of the rocky point protected the crescent scrap of beach, so she was well off before knee deep. She set to with both oars with a will, nigh onto expertly.

Yes, a proper miss yet well able to ply an oar, thank you very much. She leaned into each pull, stretching back, back. The dory's sharp bow cut through the sea like an arrow. "Practical skill," she muttered aloud. Practicality had landed her here, most assuredly.

She'd ruined her family's Christmas by steering her sister clear of one particularly dashing although likely nigh-onto criminal suitor. Everyone had liked him. Wouldn't you know?

She'd not managed to attract even one reasonable suitor for herself, what with her insistence on being too sensible. If only she could have dressed like her sister and chattered enchantingly with all the men!

She flushed, thinking back to how she'd discussed newest types of lights with Patrick. She guessed she should have acted witless and simply admired him.

At the time, he had seemed happy to explain how clarity could be effected. "Even a tiny beam can reach over impressive distances." He had showed her his various designs, as well as small, working models of the great light they were building.

She must have bored the poor man to tears! She heaved on her oars with savagery. Why hadn't she used better sense? She ought to have talked about, about…oh dear, what did her sister constantly chatter about with her admirer? Shopping? Artwork? Gossip?

Her dory, fueled by fury, flew.

The long wailing call repeated, closer. The voice seemed stationary. The victim could not be adrift, she guessed, but on the rocks. Alysa looked anxiously around, for the toothy rocks would not be kind to her vessel, either. She'd not want to fetch up on them suddenly. She'd heave her vessel to port, as soon as she could make out the dark shadow of the rocks, and let the current slow her approach.

It seemed a sensible plan.

Sensible. A sideways wave caught the nose of the dory and sent a frigid splash onto her lap. She leaned away, too late to avoid a having a whitecap come over the gunnels. She gasped as gallons of water swamped the dory. She scrambled to heave the oars and regain control, she could not that port side slip lower!

She dug in, fast. She'd got passed the protection of the rock outcropping, she guessed.

"Halloooo," she called, waiting for a response to

give her direction.

"Help," answered, more clearly, and near. Very near—and to her left.

She leaned into the oars again. "Coming," she called, hoping she sounded confident and not half as panicked as she felt.

At least the waves weren't huge. They were enough, but not storm waves. Another just barely slopped over the dory's leading edge. She could hear a fair bit of water sloshing around in the boat now. She yanked desperately on her the oar, No, it was no good at all. She'd keep the waves out, but turned off course.

Darn the darkness, she could scarcely see the pointed rocks.

A crashing wave sent the dory sideways and she struggled to get it straight again. She leaned into the oars. She'd get there, or she wouldn't.

She'd do her best and if both of them went together, at least she was not alone in this last hour. Perhaps alone most of her life, but tonight, at least one other soul stood not far off! Out of the night, a dark shape loomed. She reached out an oar, not quite believing he was real, but he seized the far end of the oar.

"Hang on!"

The man struggled into the waves. He had to scramble into the freezing water and over slick rock, likely covered with razor-sharp barnacles. She could think of naught but his pain.

"I've got you." She stretched ridiculously far forward. He plainly could not grab with any strength. She seized on his belt and heaved. He landed halfway in, along with too much sea. One more heave and he was safe. She pushed off the rock with haste, and spun the craft expertly into the surf. She'd make straight for the beach.

"Thank you," the man gasped. "Thank you."

Really, she'd failed again. Gone to sea to save one lone man, and it had to be an elderly fellow with a scruffy beard. She heaved at the oars. I must put a letter in the mail to let Mother know I've bored the one I liked and landed one too old. Landed, like a fish…she giggled. Oh dear, she was quite losing her mind.

"No light," the man gasped. "Thought I'd got beyond the point."

She craned to look backward toward the beach. Utter darkness met her gaze. Her heart sank. She might well end up crashing too.

The wind sent the waves in all directions and she couldn't clearly judge a direct route back to the beach. She listened for the surf. The waves hit the rocks beside her, and slapped loudly into her dory. Distantly they raged around the lighthouse.

Listening gave her no idea of direction.

Once more, she scanned the darkness and there, impossibly, one light twinkled.

She blinked. One single candle glimmered steadily against the dark.

"Patrick." Warmth flooded over her. He had returned; returned and come looking for her!

Who else could send out a tiny Christmas twinkler with such power?

She aimed for it. She could not doubt she must make this one, final, desperate effort. She had not the strength to continue fighting the oars forever. She leaned all her weight against the oars, three pulls, four, and at after the fifth, risked a look over her shoulder.

Yes, Patrick stood there by the water's edge! The island's stormy seas bringing us together, Alysa thought, exactly as they did for Elizabeth and Daro! Yesterday's Alysa might have doubted…

Patrick held his model light aloft as he waded into the freezing sea to meet her. "Alysa, you are the most courageous person I have ever met!"

"Your light saved us," she assured him. "It was your light. I saw it all the way out at the shoal. It gave me direction. You are simply brilliant."

"You went out there without any hope of help! I never even told you I planned to return, to bring you Christmas dinner. Alysa! You went with no idea of safety for yourself. I cannot imagine anything more courageous."

"It was your light, your brilliant design that has saved us both." She blushed furiously yet knew…she knew! His face was completely alight.

"My dear, it's no more than a light. You are a heroine."

There in the dark, soggy and freezing and the wind whipping her hair wild, she said, "It was the only practical course."

Patrick laughed out loud even as he bent to assist the older man from the dory.

Miss Ariel Grayson—yes, of the famous family— guessed she'd been right all along. At Christmas, anything could happen.

The old artist found himself assigned with yet another painting of a young couple—proving hope and joy continued, wherever it found a chance—in spite of the war.

Trouble Cove

A word about the author...

Northeastern North America is a composite of beauty and history, from north to south. Author Nancy Lindley-Gauthier has thrilled to follow the Cabot Trail by motorcycle, whale-watch at the Baie de Gaspé, and journey along the St. Lawrence Seaway. Her novel *Trouble Cove* shares a vision of lives on Cape Breton Island at the start of the twentieth century, in a time of turmoil but also of trust.

If you have enjoyed *Trouble Cove*, please visit my websites:

nlindleygauthier.wordpress.com/

http://anothershoestringadventure.weebly.com/

Thank you for purchasing
this publication of The Wild Rose Press, Inc.

If you enjoyed the story, we would appreciate your
letting others know by leaving a review.

For other wonderful stories,
please visit our on-line bookstore at
www.thewildrosepress.com.

For questions or more information
contact us at
info@thewildrosepress.com.

The Wild Rose Press, Inc.
www.thewildrosepress.com

Stay current with The Wild Rose Press, Inc.

Like us on Facebook

https://www.facebook.com/TheWildRosePress

And Follow us on Twitter
https://twitter.com/WildRosePress